"This novel is uproariously funny and will have you chuckling until the last page is turned....*Guns Will Keep Us Together* proves to be a definite keeper novel as it is one of the funniest romances I have read in a long, long time."

—Romance Reader at Heart

"Another wicked blend of action, romance, mystery, and dark humor, *Guns Will Keep Us Together* gives readers bullets, buff guys, and bad boys...I hope the Bombay family continues on with their deadly misadventures."

—Newsandsentinel.com

'SCUSE ME WHILE I KILL THIS GUY

"With an irreverent, tell-it-like-it-is, suburban-mom-assassin narrator, Leslie Langtry's *'Scuse Me While I Kill This Guy* delivers wild and wicked fun."

—Julie Kenner, *USA Today* Bestselling Author of *California Demon*

"Darkly funny and wildly over the top, this mystery answers the burning question, 'Do assassin skills and Girl Scout merit badges mix?' One truly original and wacky novel!"

—*Romantic Times BOOKreviews*

"Those who like dark humor will enjoy a look into the deadliest female assassin and PTA mom's life."

—*Parkersburg News*

"The fast-paced romantic suspense chick lit thriller is over the top, but fans will want to follow suit as Leslie Langtry provides a satirical family drama."

—*Midwest Book Reviews*

"Mixing a deadly sense of humor and plenty of sexy sizzle, Leslie Langtry creates a brilliantly original, laughter-rich mix of contemporary romance and suspense in *'Scuse Me While I Kill This Guy*."

—*Chicago Tribune*

DINNER DATE WITH DEATH

"I think we should have dinner with Arje when we get to the city," Veronica said.

"What?"

"You know, Arje Dekker? We met him at the last wrestling match. I think he was Danish or something."

"Dutch," I said absently. Now there was another problem entirely. I still had my assignment to take out Dekker. My complications had just taken on complications for themselves. "We might not even run into him." I had to discourage her from the idea of hanging out with my next target. At some point, Dekker would be dead and Ronnie would probably be somewhat pissed off about that.

"You promised." Ronnie narrowed her eyes and it sort of turned me on. Hell, everything she did turned me on lately. I might even throw my first match just to spend the rest of the festival naked in her arms—I was that desperate.

"Fine. If we see him, we can make some plans for lunch or something. But that's it."

I was grateful when she accepted this with a smile and we continued working. However, I had the sneaking suspicion it was far from over.

I Shot
You Babe

Leslie Langtry

Making
it.

NEW YORK CITY

This book is dedicated to my husband, Tom.
Cy is modeled, as are almost all my heroes, on him.

MAKING IT®

July 2009

Published by

Dorchester Publishing Co., Inc.
200 Madison Avenue
New York, NY 10016

ISBN 10: 0-8439-6291-7
ISBN 13: 978-0-8439-6291-8
E-ISBN: 978-1-4285-0697-8

The name "Making It" and its logo are trademarks of Dorchester Publishing Co., Inc.

Printed in the United States of America.

10 9 8 7 6 5 4 3 2 1

Visit us on the web at www.dorchesterpub.com.

ACKNOWLEDGMENTS

A huge, overdue, and much-deserved "thank you" to Cheryl Smith. This woman dragged me up to meet my future editor at RWA in Atlanta and forced me to pitch this series to her. Without Cheryl, who knows if the Bombays would exist in print?

Thanks, Cheryl!

I Shot
You Babe

Chapter One

"I thoroughly disapprove of duels. If a man should challenge me, I would take him kindly and forgivingly by the hand and lead him to a quiet place and kill him."

—MARK TWAIN

Okay. Stop me if you've heard this before. A pro football player walks into a bar. He falls to the floor clutching his head in pain and says, "I didn't see that coming." True story. Although maybe, just maybe, it would be more accurate to say the iron rod walked into the football player, but I'm telling it my way.

I managed to kick the guy in the ribs as he tried to get up, but one of his enormous hands (which, I assume, can only have made him good at his sport) grabbed my ankle and pulled me down to join him on the floor. It was at this point that he seemed to gain the upper hand. The lumbering side o' beef with legs climbed on top of me, bouncing my head off the cement twice. This did nothing for my self-esteem and probably wasn't good for the "rugged attractiveness" women told me I had. Did you know you actually do see stars when your head is pummeled against

1

something so unyielding as concrete? I know, it seems too cartoonish, but then, there it is.

I distracted my target by biting his forearm. I'm not fond of biting, but in this business, you have to think quickly. As he screamed, I punched him in the throat, and he crumpled over like a stack of dimes. With Vic (as in, my victim) facedown, I climbed on top and began my choke hold. Frankly, I was tired of using a choke hold. So overdone, and not terribly elegant.

Vic struggled to get free, but unfortunately for him, he was losing strength. To my surprise, he got lucky and managed to flail out, catching me (quite to his surprise) in the gut with his elbow. I dropped him and he scrambled backward until he hit the wall.

I walked toward him slowly (for dramatic effect, of course). The bastard wasn't going anywhere. Stupid athlete. They always think they can handle themselves in a fight. It was true that he was much larger than me. But it was also true that, because of this fact, he'd never really had to fight before. For his first actual battle, he was literally fighting for his life—a brilliant irony I thought would likely be wasted on him.

My fist hit him square in the face, and he slid down the wall. Through the gurgling blood coursing from his nose into his mouth just seconds before I sent the broken shards of his nose piercing into his brain, he asked, "Who are you?"

Bombay. Coney Island Bombay. Actually, you can call me Cy. I go by Coney only when I'm working as a carney. Most of the time I prefer eliminating the middle three letters from my name. It's kind of like what I really do, which is eliminating bad people.

That might sound a bit simplistic. Sorry about that. But there really is no point in analyzing it any further. I know this because I have a Ph.D. in philosophy and it has driven me to distraction most of my life. It is possible to overthink things now and then. After all, sometimes a cigar is just a cigar.

This, however, isn't one of those times. This time, the cigar is more than it seems. The rather ugly, large cigar of which I speak (who now lay lifeless on his basement floor) was a popular sports figure who ran an illegal white slave trade on the side. I've never been much of a sports fan. It seems wrong to me that professional athletes make millions of dollars when scientists trying to cure cancer and teachers educating children live from check to check. This gig was my own small contribution toward evening things out. You know, the old yin-yang thing.

My vic was a professional football player who'd invested in an Eastern European slaver. The slaver sent young women all over the world to work as prostitutes. I use the past tense because I took care of that bastard a couple of days ago. The athlete was quick to join him in death. It wasn't pretty. And honestly, I don't feel too bad about that.

Most of the Bombays tend to maintain a low profile when it comes to wet work. Making murder look like an accident seems to make them feel better. I don't really go that route. My preferred modus operandi is to actually make it appear to be foul play. And if you knew how bad these people were, you'd probably agree with me.

Two days later, the police and media seemed to think the Russian Mafia was responsible, and when the evidence I left behind revealed his crimes, Vic's jersey and status were yanked from the Pro Football Hall of Fame. My mother and the rest of the Bombay Council were pleased. Dad, an Aussie, had to call to remind me that technically my vic didn't play *real* football. But that's Pop, always splitting hairs.

My family history is interesting, in a bloodthirsty sort of way. The Bombays have cornered the market on international assassination for hire since ancient Greece. Every infant born with Bombay blood becomes a killer. We begin training at age five and progress from there. There is no way out. Once you are born a Bombay, your fate is sealed. No one rebels unless they have a suicide wish. Occasionally, someone does. What can I say? Every family has at least one idiot. Doesn't yours?

The football job took place in Chicago, and a few days later I was in Omaha. The alarm went off at six a.m., and I sat up on the edge of my bed, running my hands through my hair. You might think I'm a morning person. Nothing could be further from the truth. I'm actually more of a discipline guy. I get up to make myself functional. The exercise that follows is simply for masochistic purposes. I've been told I'm in excellent shape. It's the discipline thing.

Wheek! Wheek! came the brain-splitting cry of my

guinea pig, Sartre. The minute I wake up, she reminds me that it's time for breakfast. She's affectionate and sweet, but I've always suspected that she considers me to be little more than a servant.

"Here you are," I said as I placed a small dish of strawberries, collard greens and baby carrots in front of her. Sartre grunted and began her feast. I walked to the door of my trailer to get the paper.

When I'm on the road (which is pretty much always), I like to park my RV in Wal-Mart parking lots. They seem to have a camper cult following. At every one I've been to, there's a newspaper at my door in the morning and fresh coffee ready before the shoppers arrive. I like that. It's a nice touch.

Opening the door revealed a bright, late August. I scooped up the paper and nodded to the older woman standing in the parking lot across from me. It was then that I realized I hadn't put any clothes on. Huh. I shut the door behind me (but not before winking at the lady) and, after tossing the paper on a chair, threw on some running clothes. Ten minutes later, I opened the door to find her and several other women standing in the same place. I don't know what they hoped to see, but clearly my having clothes on had been a bit of a buzz kill. Just for fun I grinned and shouted, "G'day, ladies," with an Australian accent (something I inherited from Dad). That seemed to do the trick. I believe one actually fainted.

A good jog always helped clear my head. With my Bombay-appointed duty over for the year and the carnival season coming to an end, I had to start making my plans for fall. I was pretty sure it was time for a sabbatical. I needed a break.

Back at the trailer, Sartre squeaked indignantly. I scooped her up as I flipped on the television to listen to while I threw breakfast together. Sartre wiggled in the crook of my left arm before sprawling out luxuriously. I found an orange and made some toast while the little pig ran up and down the table. There wasn't much on in the news, as usual. I had a gig coming up in rural Nebraska. Just a county fair. Then the season would be over for me. Sartre nibbled on an orange peel, never taking her eyes off me. Huh. It's sad when your own pet doesn't entirely trust you. But that's the nature of an assassin pet owner, I guess. I gave her some of the fruit and she devoured it. An ad for Disney World came on and somehow managed to get my attention.

I clicked off the TV and pulled open my laptop. After a few more hours of research, I decided on my sabbatical: Disney World. I had a few connections there—a couple of my carney brethren who had gone legit. I flipped open my cell phone and dialed. Within moments I had a job lined up from fall to spring. After that, who knew what I'd do? I was unattached. A loner, to be clichéd—but it suited me.

Besides, I already had a career. I had travel, adventure, middle-aged women in the parking lot ogling my physique, and the love of a good, elitist rodent. What else could I possibly need?

Chapter Two

"Women: you can't live with them, and you can't get them to dress up in a skimpy Nazi uniform and beat you with a warm squash."

—EMO PHILIPS

Ah. The Saunders County Fair in Wahoo, Nebraska. The name says it all, doesn't it? Nothing but dirt, horse-shit and fried food as far as the eye can see. Sigh. It's paradise. I checked the crankshaft on the Tilt-A-Whirl before admitting sticky children and beer-addled adults to the ride. People expect a carney doesn't really give a damn when he checks the safety bars and pushes the button to start the ride. But they don't know me. I'm a firm believer in safety first, because I actually like kids. Adults, however, are more complicated.

I grinned through my beard and turned on the ride, watching as the little cars swiveled and swirled. I hadn't had a barfer in two days, but I figured I was overdue. Sure enough, when the ride came to a stop, some green-faced teen was being led off her car. It didn't bother me. When you eat five corn dogs with a cotton-candy chaser, then go on a ride that scrambles your insides like eggs, you have to expect a little carnage.

7

Oh, well. This was my last gig before heading out to Orlando. I'd have to use the solution my brilliant scientist cousin, Missi, gave me to erase the tattoos. I'd miss the beard a bit. Even though I generally lived off the grid, I was still a bit paranoid. The disguise kept me from being recognized, and the customers seemed to expect it. It came with the carney image, and I hated to disappoint anyone. I was so involved in my thoughts it took me a minute to realize the woman standing before me didn't want a ride—at least, not on the Tilt-A-Whirl.

She looked to be in her mid- to late twenties, with chin-length blonde hair, very little makeup and a slim build. I watched for a moment as she shifted her weight from one foot to the other. Definitely nervous.

"Can I help you?" I asked.

She stuck out her right hand as if she had never shaken hands before. I slowly grasped it in my own and she shook it. I could feel her heart beating in her palm. Must be the beard. It scared even Sartre.

"Um, I'm Veronica Gale." It looked as though she immediately regretted giving her last name. I took no offense. I was used to such a reaction.

"Hello, Veronica." I thought it might be rude if I didn't respond. Of course, I still had no idea why she was standing there, but I thought I should at least make her comfortable. And there was something about her. She wasn't mysterious; in fact, I could read through her like tissue paper over a large-print picture book.

"I'm finishing up my master's thesis on transient lifestyles and wondered if I could interview you?" Ms. Gale bit her lip, displaying a lack of confidence that I found a little adorable.

Ah. So that was it. An academic. You don't see many in this line of work. I felt a twinge of nostalgia for the ivory tower.

"Okay." I stepped past her and admitted more kids to the ride. "I've got a break in an hour."

Veronica jumped back as if she hadn't noticed the people around her. "Um, fine. I'll be back in an hour." She paused for a second, as if her central nervous system had failed her. Finally she turned around and marched off.

Hmmm. A sheltered little thing with no life experience and plenty of attitude. How could I possibly resist? And who was I to stand in the way of a fellow academic and her quest for knowledge?

I checked all the safety bars and switched on the ride. I didn't really have a break coming up, so I called one of the other guys on duty on my radio. Mort agreed to cover for me in a bit.

I was actually looking forward to talking to Veronica Gale, master's candidate. I hadn't had a date in a long time. Sure, carneys have followers—often wealthy housewives with a sexual fetish for tattooed flesh—but a real date? It was too depressing to think about. As I said, I'm a loner, but that doesn't mean I don't get lonely for intelligent conversation with a woman. Most of my contact included very little discussion.

Mort showed up less than an hour later. When my "date" arrived a few seconds after, I suggested we hit the beer tent. We bought two drinks and settled at a splinter-riddled picnic table.

Veronica slid her beer to the side and pulled a notebook out of her purse. I smiled. She was starting to grow on me.

"Now, your name is . . . ?" she asked, sounding very official. This chick had to loosen up.

"Coney Bombay." I watched as she wrote that down. She had beautiful, slender fingers. I like that in a woman. Veronica Gale wasn't a hottie. She was pretty in an interesting sort of way, with large, questioning green eyes, a classic European nose, a strong chin and dark blonde hair. I found her intriguing. I'd like to think she found me intriguing, but then I remembered her nervousness around me. To her, I was just some sort of hobo who still had all his teeth.

"Thank you for agreeing to talk to me, Mr. Bombay." All friendliness had gone from her voice. This woman was pure business now. At least, that was what she wanted me to think.

"Call me Cy. And no problem. This is the best proposition I've had all day." I smiled, hoping to loosen her up.

It didn't. Veronica scowled. "Fine. Cy it is. But this is not a proposition."

"Too bad," I responded, never taking my eyes off of hers. It unnerved her. Have you ever tried to keep your eyes on the person you are talking to? Americans aren't used to it. They look away every now and then to fight their unease. Especially when you are a carney. Veronica was no exception.

"All right. What do you want to know regarding my . . . what was it? Transient lifestyle?" Hmmm . . . when you added the word *lifestyle* it made me sound like a hobo sporting platform sandals and lime green eye shadow.

"How long have you been employed by the . . ." Ms. Gale stumbled over her words in what appeared to be an attempt at political correctness. "Um . . ."

"How long have I been a carney?" I stepped in to rescue her. Now, why did I do that? I certainly didn't owe this woman an explanation of my chosen profession. "Almost twelve years now. I've worked with a number of outfits—this one for two years."

"And what did you do before that?"

"I was a student." Actually, I still considered myself to be a student. But for the sake of this interview, I thought I'd keep it simple.

Veronica looked me in the eyes. She didn't seem to believe that twelve years ago I was in high school. I could've helped her out, but I held back.

"How old are you?" she asked. Clearly, this woman wasn't one for social graces. I couldn't figure out why that was. Usually I'm good at reading people. But was she asking me as a researcher or out of her own personal curiosity?

"I'm thirty-eight." I could see her doing the math in her head. Eventually the question would come up, and it would confuse her. For some reason, I wanted to let her off the hook. What was wrong with me? I could see Sartre rolling her eyes back in her cage in the trailer.

"I have a postgraduate degree in philosophy. I spent most of my twenties in school. Like you," I answered before she asked.

"Like me? What do you mean?" Veronica sat straight up.

I leaned forward and looked her in the eyes again. "Correct me if I'm wrong, but you appear to be about twenty-six or so. My guess is that you have been in school ever since kindergarten. I'm also guessing you'll go for your Ph.D. as soon as you are through with your thesis."

I expected her to be angry. Hell, I expected her to throw her beer in my face and walk off. She didn't.

"Is it that easy to see?" Her question was strangely straightforward.

I shook my head. "No. It just takes one to know one. I did the same thing until I ran out of degrees. Then I ran away and joined the carnival."

Veronica sighed as if she'd been holding her breath all this time. She actually reached for her beer and drained half the cup. I waited.

"Did your family harass you about it too?" She seemed to ask the question with some degree of bitterness. The tide was turning in my favor.

"No. They didn't really mind. They weren't even surprised when I became a carney." That is actually true. The Bombays don't care what your cover is. It's merely important to have one. Well, unless you became an attorney. Then they'd probably kill you outright.

I kind of expected Veronica to see my admission as heartening—something that would inspire her to give me her life story. She didn't.

"So why did you take your education and throw it away for this?" She gestured around her. Did I detect disgust in her voice? How boring.

"Why not? I can't see a better place to examine the human soul." I folded my arms.

My interviewer snorted. "Well, Cy, it seems like a waste to me."

So that was how it was going to be, eh?

"Tell me, Ms. Gale, what practical applications does your thesis have for everyday life?"

Her eyes snapped to mine. Gone was the brief vulnerability I'd seen earlier. I'd pissed her off. Oddly enough, I liked it.

"I don't have to explain my intellectual interests to you!" Ooh. A defiant outburst. How original.

"But you are asking me to do that. Aren't you?" I adopted a more distant tone. For a moment, I'd thought maybe this woman had something more to offer. Instead, she was just another overeducated snob.

"Let's just keep this professional, Mr. Bombay."

"Fine."

She looked back at her notepad. "So, why do you choose to live outside the norms expected by society?"

"I see it as an apprenticeship for a future career in the entertainment industry."

Her eyes grew wide. "Seriously? That's interesting. What do you want to do?" Ms. Gale began to scribble on her notepad.

"I want to be a Henry Kissinger impersonator. That's where the real money is."

Veronica narrowed her eyes. "That's not funny."

I ignored her. "But first, I have to work on my condescending attitude. Maybe you can give me some pointers."

She started to pack up her stuff.

"Of course, the Kissinger thing might be a bit overdone these days. In that case I'll have to fall back on my dream of studying the effects of business cards on giant, hissing cockroaches."

She rose to her feet.

"Now, my cousin, she's got some really lofty goals. She wants to drive an ice-cream truck. You should talk with her."

"Thank you for the interview. I appreciate it."

"Was it something I said?" I clutched my chest dramatically.

Veroncia Gale turned a lovely shade of red as she spun on her heel and left me. No sense of humor in that one.

Later that night as we packed up the carnival and I said good-bye to my friends for the last time, I couldn't help wondering what would become of Veronica Gale.

I'd given her some information she could use. Unfortunately, she would end up a dull college professor with no experience in real life. But I couldn't help that. After all, Disney World and Sartre beckoned, and it was time to begin a new chapter in the life of Cy Bombay, carney/assassin.

Chapter Three

"I think crime pays. The hours are good, you travel a lot."

—WOODY ALLEN

The plain brown envelope was hand-delivered by my cousin Paris during spring break. He was at Disney World with his sister, Liv, and her family, along with my cousins Dak and Gin and their families. Paris and Dak were on a job, unbeknownst to their sisters, and I was pretty sure Dak didn't even know Paris was ferrying an assignment from the Bombay Council to me. That's the way things work in this family. Everything is kept on a need-to-know basis.

I ripped open the envelope. Another job. Who would it be? A drug kingpin? Mafia? Serial killer? It didn't really matter, because he'd be dead shortly. No point standing on ceremony.

Inside was another envelope—this one with a note from Mum with little hearts drawn on it. Apparently, I'm still her "little Squidgy." That was somewhat comforting. I dropped her note in Sartre's cage and she immediately began to shred it.

The arrogant face of a man named Fred Reid stared up at me. Why did I always get the big guys? Mr. Reid looked to be about 265 pounds, maybe six-foot-four. At any rate, he was much bigger than I am. While I used to not mind a challenge, in a couple of years I'd be forty and not as spry as I used to be.

According to the dossier, Freddie was the son of the English ambassador to the United States. Beyond possessing a keen understanding of the words *diplomatic immunity*, Fred was nothing more than an ignorant thug. He'd been picked up on numerous occasions for attempted murder and selling and buying narcotics, and was the top suspect in a number of cold cases, many of which included the murder of people who were supposed to testify against him. Oh, I was going to have fun with this one.

Vic was scheduled to appear at a fund-raiser in Miami with his father in two days. Not much time to prepare, and I was scheduled to work at Disney World. While that never stopped me before, I did believe in professional commitment. And I liked running the Kali River Rapids ride. Unfortunately, taking out the vic came first. Finding a replacement at Disney wouldn't be tough. It helped to be wealthy enough to bribe coworkers. And since many were college students, finding a replacement was even easier if I threw in a bottle of booze. I always made it the good stuff, because I remembered the crap I used to drink in college. There's nothing like a little Grey Goose vodka to break up the monotony between Mogen David and Lancers.

The drive to Miami was nice. Sartre chattered the

whole time, indignant about having to leave the trailer behind in Orlando. It was like a giant playpen for her. But I needed to be in the chichi hotel where my vic stayed in order to make it work, and I didn't want to leave her with someone else. Besides, I liked the companionship, even if the conversation was a bit one-sided.

Sartre calmed down when I gave her some fresh spinach leaves to munch on. I only wished women were that easy.

The Miami Del Rey was located on prime beach-front property. The pink Art Deco building stood out among the more modern high-rises. A five-star hotel, the Del Rey was known for its obliging staff, which catered to the wealthy and spoiled. I loved these places—you know the type—where they didn't have a reservation desk because that would be too gauche. Instead, there was a woman sitting at a small table in an obscure corner of the lobby. She gave me my room key and made arrangements to have my luggage transferred to my room. She also slipped me her phone number. Sigh.

I reached the door to my room with no problem. Sartre was obediently quiet in my satchel and raised no alarms. She'd been through this drill before. Once inside the room, I unpacked my things, including a collapsible cage for the pig—something I designed myself.

The file included the various peccadilloes of my vic, along with his schedule. Tomorrow was the fund-raiser, but Reid had the bad habit of not showing up for such events. Miami was a city crawling with vice, and with his love for gambling and—I did *not* make this up—"gender illusionists," my guess was that Reid would be otherwise occupied that evening.

Which left tonight to do the job. Using a cheap, pay-as-you-go cell phone, I called the front desk and asked for Reid's room. They connected me and I started the trace on my laptop. His room number came up almost immediately, thanks to my cousin Missi, who had come up with this particular technology a few months back. It looked just like a memory stick with a kitten hanging from a branch and the words *Hang in There* on it.

I changed into a nondescript black suit and headed up to Reid's room. Walking past to make sure I wasn't being watched, I slipped back to the room and knocked on the door. Upon hearing no answer, I slid my all-purpose room card into the slot and was rewarded with a click as the door popped open.

Once inside, I quickly checked the room for surveillance cameras and, finding none, began to search for ideas that would help me take this bastard out. It would have been easy to hide and wait for his return, but it was obvious that more than one person shared the room.

I was running out of time. I needed to find something that would tip me off to his whereabouts or plans. It only made sense to kill him outside the hotel. That would take suspicion off of me.

Footsteps in the corridor made my heart beat a bit faster. This was an adrenaline rush, not fear. I didn't believe in fear—it only made things worse. A key card slid through the slot. I had only a split second to dive into the bathroom and close the door.

Someone was moving about the room, opening drawers and turning the TV on and off. I heard nothing for a few moments. Had he gone? I waited—not an easy thing to do in a hotel shower. I hated hiding. Personally, I preferred the direct approach. Less bullshit and more fun.

After ten more minutes of examining the tiles for mildew, I gave up. Vic must have left. Even so, I slipped noiselessly from the shower and opened the bathroom door. As I started across the bedroom, I heard a cell phone ring. I froze. It was then that I noticed my vic stretched out on the bed, oblivious to me as he answered his phone.

I remained where I was, frozen like a statue. Vic was babbling some nonsense on the phone. I was certainly in his peripheral vision. You'd think he would notice a strange blond man in a black suit standing in midstride just a few yards to his left. I'd like to think I'd notice something like that. It gave me a few seconds to think about how I could kill him.

Looking around without moving my head was a new experience for me. The room was devoid of heavy statuary, .45s with silencers (that would have been too convenient, I suppose), or even a letter opener. I had nothing on me—this was just meant to be a surveillance job. Well, I had my passkey room card, but what could I do with that besides give him a nasty plastic cut? There wasn't enough time to wait for his cell phone to give him brain cancer, and the landline phone wasn't big enough to bash him in the head.

Vic clicked off the phone, and that was when he noticed me standing there. Thank God too, because I was getting sick of acting like I was frozen in time. The funny thing was, he just lay there on the bed. Maybe he was blind?

I couldn't be so lucky. He hurled the cell phone at me. I guess he could see after all. I dodged the high-tech Treo as it smashed into the wall and into a million little shiny pieces. Technology today.

I reached for the lamp on the nightstand, only to find it was bolted down. Fantastic. It gave Vic just enough time to regain his senses and spring from the bed—a feat that impressed me, considering his size. I was even more impressed when he landed a ham-fisted punch to the side of my head.

Bringing my knee up, I connected with his groin, groaning at his lack of foresight. Most men expect that kind of contact and block it. Not this idiot. He actually began to whimper the word *Mommy* over and over. The two of us stumbled a little, him with swelling testicles and me with a bit of a concussion. Instead of stars, for some reason I saw the kitten on the memory stick Missi had given me. After regaining my senses, I dragged his doubled-up body to the terrace. Vic groaned as I pushed open the French doors and looked over the edge of his private veranda. It was about six stories down to the pool. If I managed it just right, I'd be out the door and in the stairwell before he smashed into the concrete just to the left of the pool.

Vic was still in a fetal position. What a loser. I wished all my vics fell so easily. He was heavy, but I managed to get him to the low fence at least before he rallied and decided he didn't fancy a swim.

The son of a bitch landed a pretty strong kick to my shin, and it stopped me in my tracks long enough for him to rise to his feet. Good. It would be much easier to shove him over the railing if he was standing. With a running start I barreled into his abdomen with my shoulder and he went over like a Slinky. I didn't wait to see what happened. His scream told me he was on his way down and I was overdue in my own room. After a brief stop to wipe down everything I'd touched, I fled the scene of the crime.

"That did not go well," I informed Sartre as I returned to my room. She looked at me sideways to indicate that that was *exactly* what she expected from me and went back to munching on a carrot. Since she was of no help whatsoever, I stripped off my clothes and looked in the mirror.

My face was red and starting to swell, and my right shin was bleeding. I used styptic powder to stop the blood and opened my shaving kit. Missi had invented a sort of steroid that when injected stopped the bruising process in its tracks. When I traveled, I kept the solution in bottles labeled, *Insulin*. No one ever questioned me.

The steroid would take about half an hour to work, which meant I couldn't leave the room until then. Killing Vic in the hotel made for an interesting dilemma. The authorities could launch a room-by-room search, and unless there had just been a recent rash of brawling, I'd be the only patron who looked like he'd been in a life-or-death struggle.

Sirens blared outside and I knew it would be only a matter of time. The question was: Should I stay or should I go?

Chapter Four

"The very existence of flamethrowers proves that sometime, somewhere, someone said to themselves, 'You know, I want to set those people over there on fire, but I'm just not close enough to get the job done.'"

—GEORGE CARLIN

After an hour, curiosity drove me out of the shower and into a pair of linen trousers and a silk shirt. I needed a little intel on the situation and figured I'd get it where most people did—from a bartender. I know, you thought it was more cloak-and-dagger than that, didn't you? It may be hard to believe, but bartenders have been my most important sources for years. I remember this one time in Ireland when I was being stalked by these IRA operatives. I'd be dead right now if a bartender named Paddy hadn't let me know I was about to leave the bar with the service unit director's girlfriend.

Back in Miami, the bar was called FIVE, and the bartender was called Arturo. It was pretty crowded, and I could tell that the "accident" had caused a lot of problems for the hotel. Sorry about that.

Arturo opened up easily when I waved the hundred-dollar tip in his face. All he knew was that the manager said some VIP had fallen from the balcony and the place was crawling with State Department flunkies. I decided to stay put for a while. Besides, they had an excellent scotch selection and I had a front-row seat to the madness.

"Twenty dollars for a Chablis?" I heard the blonde next to me complain. "Are you serious?"

I knew that voice immediately. I slid the money to Arturo and he took the hint and handed the lady a Chablis.

"What? I didn't order this!"

I hoped Arturo wouldn't rat me out.

"The gentleman did," I heard him say. Thanks.

"Well." The woman turned around to face me. "No, thank you."

I couldn't help but smile. "Please, Ms. Gale. I never could resist a damsel in distress."

Veronica Gale froze before me. "How did you know my name?" She clutched her purse, eyeing me nervously. She looked good. Really good. This little academic drone cleaned up nicely in a revealing, yet plain little black dress and three-inch heels.

I held out my right hand. "Allow me to reintroduce myself. Coney Bombay." I watched with amusement as recognition fought with logic across that cute face of hers.

"You . . . you're that carney . . ." Veronica stuttered.

It amused me that she was so flustered. "How did you . . . ? What are you . . . ?" She seemed to be completely incapable of ending a sentence.

"Tell you what," I started as I pushed the glass of wine back at her. "Take a deep breath and I'll explain it over dinner."

Ronnie—Veronica just begged for a nickname—picked up her glass and drained it in one swallow. I'd never seen a woman do that before—in fact, I was pretty sure she'd never done that before. And I found it somewhat arousing.

"I can't afford a drink here. What makes you think I can afford dinner?"

I signaled Arturo, who picked up the phone to make the reservation immediately.

"It doesn't really matter, does it? After all, I'm buying." I stood and guided her by the elbow to the elevator that would take us to the Parisian—the exclusive rotating restaurant at the top of the hotel. Veronica never said a word. She just stared at me as though she was still trying to work out what a guy like me was doing in a five-star hotel. I kind of liked that.

"What are the odds we would run into each other again?" I asked once we were seated in the plush chocolate-velvet booth.

"I'd say one million to one." She attempted a smile. It was hard to tell whether she was happy to see me or not.

"And yet here we are." I placed the white linen napkin across my lap and ordered a bottle of white wine.

In French. Yes, I wanted to impress her. I had no idea why.

"Yes. Here we are." Veronica looked around, and I wondered if she had changed her mind about having dinner with me.

"Well, thank you for accepting my invitation. I'd be willing to bet seeing me was something of a shock."

The sommelier arrived and opened the wine. He poured a small amount and I tasted it. After I nodded my approval, he poured for both of us.

After a few sips, Veronica hiccuped (rather charmingly, I might add). "This is a lot different from the drink we shared last year."

"Yes, I suppose so."

"So why are you here?"

"Sick friend. A carney. You'd like him."

"Why's that?" she asked.

"He doesn't have any teeth."

Veronica sighed. "I guess I deserved that. I'm sorry I was so rude last year. I shouldn't put labels on people."

"Apology accepted. So why are you here?" I volleyed.

She squirmed uneasily in her chair. "Conference. I'm presenting my thesis."

"I'd like to see that."

"I already gave it this morning."

The waiter arrived and took our orders. We sized each other up for a moment.

"I should apologize also," I said. "I was a bit rough on you."

She nodded. "Yes, you were. I like what I'm doing. I love school." She flung her arms up. "Why does everyone find that upsetting?"

"Who is everyone?"

"My family, my friends, the faculty. They all think I need to take some time off and go somewhere. See stuff. Do things."

"I would agree with that."

"Why?"

"Because I was like you. I stayed in college for eight years. I did some traveling here and there"—mainly to kill people, but no need to mention that—"but I always returned to my ivory tower."

Her eyes changed. No, the look in her eyes changed. She had a faint recognition within those green depths.

"Why did you leave the university?"

Was she really interested?

"Because the minute I got my Ph.D., they offered me a teaching post. It scared the hell out of me. In that moment I saw my body aging while standing in the same place over the years. I saw the same people around me, the same city, saw myself teaching the same kind of students over and over. And I didn't like it."

Veronica shook her head. "I don't understand. It sounds wonderful to me."

Our food arrived. The sommelier wisely brought another bottle of wine and poured. Veronica watched with hungry eyes. I'd forgotten that she was a student. Most likely a dead-broke one. I wondered how she could even afford the hotel . . . unless the university was footing the bill.

"So you became a carney? And now you can afford all this? I don't get it."

I smiled and tucked into my steak. It was amazing— medium-rare. Just the way I like it.

She giggled without waiting for my reply. "I shouldn't drink this much. I rarely drink at home." And then she guzzled another glass of wine.

"Well, enjoy it. I want you to."

We didn't speak while we attacked our food as genteelly as possible. I was starving. The fight with Vic had taken a lot out of me, and I hadn't had the heart to devour Sartre's fruit-and-veggie cache.

After half an hour, Veronica sat back and sighed. "That was the best dinner I've had in a long, long time."

"I'm glad you enjoyed it." I grinned. I love to see women eat. It is so boring to see girls nibble at salads all the time.

"It was delicious. And the wine was excellent." She leaned across the table. "Would you mind if I ask you a personal question?"

"I'm all yours," I said, a little more truthfully than she probably imagined.

"How can you afford this hotel? This dinner?" She was blunt. It was adorable.

"I manage."

"You must have really done something with your plans as a Kissinger impersonator." She grinned.

I laughed. "And I get dental too."

"But seriously . . ." Veronica wasn't letting me off the hook. It must be that Midwestern say-what-you-think mentality. It reminded me of Australians and Dad.

"I inherited some money." And that was all I was going to say about that.

"Must be nice," she responded with a smile. Pushing her plate away, she looked up at me. "I'm done. What should we do now?"

I leaned in. "What about the fund-raiser? Isn't there somewhere you have to be?"

"No, tonight's banquet was called off. Somebody died here or something. I guess he was supposed to speak."

"How awful." I didn't really mean it. I felt like a hero for saving her from a boring speech and a rubber-chicken dinner. Killing this vic saved my lady fair.

"Yeah. Some diplomat's kid."

I divided the remaining wine into our two glasses and tried to ask as nonchalantly as possible, "How did he die?"

"No one has said, but the consensus is that he had an accident."

My cell phone vibrated in my pocket, as if on cue. I took it out and checked the screen.

"If you'll excuse me for a moment, Veronica, I have

to take this." I left the table before she had the opportunity to ask me what kind of calls a carney would get that would interrupt dinner.

I found a nice, quiet corner and answered. "Hello, Mum."

"Squidgy!" Mom shouted with enthusiasm. "Nice work!"

"Tell him it's all over the news!" I heard my dad shout in the background.

Mom mumbled something at him, then returned to me. "Anyway, well-done. And word is you helped Paris and Dak with their assignment. You're such a good boy." I could actually feel her fingers closing on my cheeks.

"Thanks, Mum. Anything else?"

"No, why?" she asked, as if anything was important enough to tear her little boy away from her.

"I'm on a date."

Mom promptly exploded. "You *are*? Oh, Squidgy! How wonderful!" I heard her mumble something to Dad about grandchildren.

"Mum, I've got to get back." I didn't want Veronica to run off.

"Okay! Have fun!" I thought I heard her say, "Get married," but that might have been my imagination.

I returned to the table and joined Veronica. "Sorry about that. Now, where were we?"

"Who was it?" Ronnie asked. I found her complete lack of tact refreshing. I really did.

"My sick friend. He's rallied. He says hello."

"Hmmm." She rolled her eyes. "I'll bet he did."

"Are you drunk?"

"Of course not." She wobbled indignantly. "I'm just a little buzzed. That's all."

Veronica stood. Then she toppled back into her chair, giggling. "Oops." She giggled again.

I liked it. But I was concerned that she'd had a bit too much to drink. And for some reason, I was pretty sure that Veronica Gale wasn't much of a drinker.

I motioned for the check, and within a few minutes I was leading one tipsy anthropologist back to where she *thought* her room might be. All I had wanted to do was loosen her up. But if this woman got any looser I was afraid her head would come off.

Chapter Five

Lieutenant John Chard: The army doesn't like more than one disaster in a day.
Bromhead: Looks bad in the newspapers and upsets civilians at their breakfast.

—*Zulu*

Thirty minutes later I was convinced Veronica had no idea where her room was. And to tell you the truth, I was getting a little worried. The hallways were filled with suits—men I assumed were from various government agencies. And they noticed that I was dragging a drunk woman around with me aimlessly through the hallways.

"Excuse me, sir." A tight-lipped man in a boring black suit asked for the seventh time, "Are you lost?"

"No, I—" I was cut off completely as Veronica launched herself into my arms and kissed me. It was nice. I enjoyed it. Maybe not half as much as the federal retinue watching us. Against my will, I came up for air.

"I'm taking her to our room right now," I answered as Veronica burst into another fit of giggles.

"Yes! We're goin' to our room!" she shouted enthusiastically.

Once inside my room, I locked the door and looked out the peephole. No one there. That was good.

"So, what now, sailor?" Veronica flopped drunkenly onto my bed and promptly passed out.

"What now, indeed." I sighed. Very carefully, I removed her shoes and dress. For a moment I felt guilty staring at her in her underwear. She really was a lovely young woman—slender and shapely. Too bad she was also something I didn't like in a woman . . . unconscious.

After covering her up, I sat in a chair by the door, watching her and listening for any movement outside. My thoughts drifted to the memories of women past. If I were a gentleman, I'd say there weren't many. Of course, then I wouldn't be a gentleman because I'd be lying. No, I'd had my fair share of women over the years. Nothing permanent since, well, since Frannie Smith. I liked to keep things detached.

It just wasn't in me to find one partner and settle down. I liked living off-the-cuff. And I guess if you think about it, I was already in a monogamous relationship with a guinea pig.

Sartre squeaked as if she knew I was thinking about her. I pulled her out of the cage and onto my lap. She snuggled up, and I stroked her fur as she purred and fell asleep. Great. I couldn't seem to keep any women awake.

There was one meaningful relationship in my sordid past. Shutting my eyes couldn't make the memory of one Frances Smith go away. The pain that stabbed my heart was just as fresh as the day she said good-bye. Frannie. She broke my heart.

Isn't there always one love who can take your heart and give it a slow, painful death? Nothing ever eased the ache. Leaning back and closing my eyes, I allowed the inevitable wash of college memories to flow. It's funny how your brain disobeys you. I didn't want to think about that. Fortunately, Sartre sank her teeth into my flesh and it all went away, dissolved in a mist of pain.

That was the pig's way of letting me know she had to pee. And since I didn't want to get soaked, I decided to put her back in her cage. I threw in a few carrots and sat back down in the chair, willing myself to sleep.

I didn't sleep much. Sitting up in a chair, fully clothed, will do that to you. Morning slipped through the sheer curtains, stealing across Veronica's face. She looked like she was lost. She kind of was, just didn't know it.

I decided to grab a quick shower. As I stepped out into the room wearing nothing but a towel, Veronica suddenly sat straight up. This time, she looked terrified.

"Oh, God. Oh, no! We didn't . . . did we?" The blanket slipped from her chest and she clawed at it to cover herself.

I smiled. "What? You don't remember?" Technically, I wasn't lying. Granted, there was a certain amount of sordid innuendo there, but I really hadn't confirmed anything.

Her eyes widened. I hoped it was more that she regretted not remembering a night of passion with me. However, it appeared she was more concerned that she'd actually had a night of passion. This woman was uptight indeed.

"Relax," I said. "You were so drunk we couldn't find your room, so I brought you here. Nothing happened." Now, why did I say that? I could've had a good time with this.

"Oh," she said. Did I detect a note of regret? Or was that what I wanted to hear?

I tossed her the big, fluffy hotel robe, and she slid into it and dashed for the bathroom.

"What are you doing?" she asked a few moments later as she stepped out of the bathroom. Her hair was smoothed, face washed and teeth brushed. I wondered if she used my toothbrush. It wouldn't have bothered me if she did. A germaphobe I ain't.

I looked down at the yarn and needles in my lap. "Knitting."

"You knit?" She seemed shocked.

"Yes." I held up the scarf I was working on. It was a lovely café-au-lait baby alpaca. I have to admit, I'm a bit of a yarn snob. Only the best will do.

Veronica reached out and touched the scarf, fondling the fibers. It was a definite turn-on.

"It's beautiful," she whispered, and pointed to the

curving rows that ran through it. "What are these things called?"

"Cables," I answered. "They thicken the fabric, and I like the way they look."

"You told me you're working in Florida. Why are you knitting a wool scarf?"

"I've got a trip coming up."

I wondered why she didn't press me for more information. Maybe she wasn't that curious when it came to me.

"I think it's cool that you knit," she said with a lopsided smile. Damn, it looked good on her.

"Thanks. It's kind of my form of meditation."

"Like yoga?"

"No, more like Buddhism." That was true. I found working with yarn and needles very soothing. It gave me something to do while I thought about whatever I wanted to think about. Knitting was something of a Bombay family tradition, although to the best of my knowledge I was the only man who did it. That didn't bother me.

"Well, I guess I'd better get back to my room," Veronica said abruptly.

I nodded. "I'll walk you there."

"You don't have to. I may have forgotten last night, but I know where it is now."

"I insist. Besides, I want my bathrobe back."

She cocked her head to one side. "I was just going to put on my dress from last night."

"Then everyone from your conference who sees you will know what you were up to last night. At least in a robe, they might figure you've just been for a morning swim."

A look of fear spread across her face. She nodded and I picked up my keys and led her to the door.

I started laughing exactly one minute and thirty-four seconds later.

"What?" she asked as she reddened.

"Come on! You are two doors down from me. And you couldn't remember that?" I chuckled and followed her into her room.

"I had a lot to drink," she said, not a little defensively.

As I wandered around her room, Veronica grabbed a pair of jeans and a T-shirt and disappeared into the bathroom.

She was a slob. Not in a bad way, just kind of messy. There were no half-empty pizza boxes, but papers and files were strewn haphazardly about the room. The phone rang and I jumped, knocking over a stack of papers.

Damn. I knelt down and began picking them up. I couldn't help but notice that this wasn't research for her anthropological thesis.

"What happened?" Veronica knelt beside me and I could smell soap and shampoo. Lavender. Very nice. She must have taken the world's fastest shower.

"Sorry." I indicated the papers. "Your phone rang and I inadvertently knocked this stuff over."

She grinned. "You? Clumsy? That's outstanding."

"Enjoy it. You won't likely see it again."

Veronica laughed, and even though it was at my expense, I liked it.

"So what is all this?" I held up a piece of paper with forensic information on it.

"Oh, um, just a pet project. It's nothing." She grabbed for the paper and started shoving as much as she could into the folder.

I pointed to a photo I recognized. "Hey, isn't this Senator Anderson?"

She frowned. "You recognize him?"

"I do keep in touch with the world. Of course I know who he is. I think most Americans do."

Senator Will Anderson had been a maverick up-and-coming Democrat. A fire-and-brimstone type, he dominated the political scene, going after corrupt politicians. Everyone seemed to like him. His name was brought up often as a potential presidential hopeful.

"He was found dead of a heart attack, right?" I asked as I handed her the picture.

Ronnie frowned at it. There was something more to her expression than just regret that his life ended too soon.

"I worked on his campaign all through college. He was amazing." She looked at me with a nervous grin, then shoved the photo into the file. My stomach clenched just a bit. I ignored it.

"So why do you have a four-inch-thick file on him in your hotel room? He died four years ago."

"It's just a hobby of mine."

"Politicians who die before their time are a hobby for you?"

"You wouldn't understand."

"Try me."

Veronica sighed heavily, as if exhaling years of pent-up frustration. "I've always believed that foul play was involved."

I nodded. "I've heard that theory too. In fact, isn't there some sort of cult following of people who think there was a government conspiracy involved?"

She looked angry. "There's a lot that doesn't add up. It would be disrespectful to ignore the evidence."

"So, this is like the Kennedy assassination conspiracy?"

"Someday we might actually know who was on the grassy knoll that day!"

I knew who was on the grassy knoll. It was something the Bombays learned early in their training. Well, that and how to hog-tie a vic using four twist ties.

I held up my hands to stave off an attack. "Okay, I'm sorry. I tend to play devil's advocate sometimes. Mea culpa."

Veronica studied me for a moment before responding. "No, I'm sorry. I'm just a bit sensitive about this." She tossed the file on the bed. "I thought he was going to change the world."

"A lot of people did. So you carry this huge file with you everywhere you go?"

"I feel like I'm getting close to finding something.

Every time I reread this stuff, I find something I didn't notice before." She shook her head. "You probably think it's stupid."

"No. I think it's admirable. And I'd like to be so lucky as to have a beautiful woman like you trying to avenge me. Even if I did die of a heart attack."

"I'm not sure that's a compliment." She didn't say anything for a moment. "I've got to get back to the conference. I've missed one seminar already, and the university is paying my way."

I took the hint. "No problem. I have to check out today anyway." I walked to the door and stopped as I opened it. "It was great to see you again, Ronnie." I noted the stoic look on her face as I left her standing there and returned to my room and the guinea pig who loved me.

Chapter Six

"Clothes make the man. Naked people have little or no influence in society."

—MARK TWAIN

A month had gone by, and the feds decided that my Miami vic had been drunk and fallen accidentally to his death. The State Department complained, but there wasn't enough to go on. Vic's father, the diplomatic envoy to the United States, resigned. All was well.

Things were going okay. Spring was ending and so was my contract at Disney World, and my scarf was finished. I had places to go and things to do.

One of my hobbies, in addition to knitting, is the study of hand-to-hand combat from other countries. I already had black belts in kung fu and aikido, and I tried to travel and train whenever possible.

I would pick a remote spot, live there for a few months, observe their techniques and try them out. I've studied pencak cilat in Indonesia; karate in Okinawa, Zulu stick fighting and kickboxing in India.

My latest plan was to hit the *Naadam* Festival in Ulaanbaatar, Mongolia. I was hoping to compete in wrestling and archery. And maybe learn some new technique in the process. In my line of work, I appreciate any tricks I can get. And the philosopher in me loved exploring the innate desire men have to fight one another.

Mongolia, even in the summer, can be cold as hell. Even in the Gobi Desert. Especially in the Gobi Desert. Hence the alpaca scarf.

Since last fall, I'd been working out at a local gym, perfecting my wrestling moves. It was tougher to practice archery and horseback riding, but I found a couple of stables that reluctantly allowed me to do it. My strongest effort would be the wrestling.

Everything was in place. Sartre and I would fly to L.A. (I knitted a little bag to take her in using buffalo yarn so she'd be cozy), then take the Bombay family private jet to Ulaanbaatar. We'd stay for a few weeks to prep, hook up with our guides and train. Sartre could hang out, munching on the grasses of the steppe while I got my ass kicked over and over in the competition. I couldn't wait.

As I spent the last few days getting organized, I couldn't help wondering what had happened to Veronica Gale. I hadn't heard from her. Not that I'd expected her to call, but I thought maybe I'd hear something. I'd left her my e-mail address and cell number. Still, I'd never really invited her to contact me.

The strange thing was, it really bothered me that she didn't call or write. And the fact that it bothered me, bothered me. I'd never wanted attachments before. So why now? Why here? Maybe I was getting old and afraid of living alone? There was something about her I found intriguing. More so than any other woman since, well, since a long time ago.

I put those thoughts aside and finished getting organized. There were a lot of arrangements to be made. Fortunately, Sansar-Huu in Manzushir Khiid was handling a lot over there. I'd sent him my measurements for my *zodag*, *shuudag* and *gutals* (or boots), the uniform I'd be wearing. Or should I say, I'd be barely wearing. The outfit resembled a purple Speedo and a pair of silk sleeves attached to resemble a barely there bolero jacket. I'd learned that the reason the jacket was so open across the chest was to discourage women from secretly entering the contest by pretending to be men. Frankly, I'd like to see that. I was hoping at least one or two women would give it a try.

Sansar-Huu had also managed to find me a true *tahki*, or Mongolian pony, for the competition. These horses were descended from the original horses used by Genghis Khan as he took over Asia and Europe. I had a thing for Genghis Khan. I'd written my master's thesis on how such a violent man peacefully embraced people of all races, religions and cultures. Of all the countries I'd visited over the years, this one was special.

I didn't think I stood a good chance of winning. But that wasn't the point. The point was to throw my hat into the arena and give it a shot. By heading out now, in the beginning of June, I'd have a little over a month for training (which, of course, wouldn't be enough) and be able to participate in the smaller, local *naadams* before the main festival in Ulaanbaatar. I was looking forward to visiting my friends again. In fact, I hadn't been back in fifteen years. But I had kept up my language lessons after leaving the Ivy League. For several years I had a carney colleague who was second-generation Mongolian. Chudruk kept me on my toes language-wise. He had since moved back to the homeland of his parents. His father was a former *naadam* champion, and I hoped to learn something from him.

The day I left, my cousin Missi came through with Veronica's personal e-mail address. That kind of research wasn't my thing. But Missi could find an amoeba in a mountain. I'd have to remember to pick her up something special from my trip.

So I sent Veronica an e-mail. It was simple, just inquiring how she was doing and mentioning that I would be in her area at the end of the summer. I got a reply back immediately.

Veronica Gale is out of town for the summer. Please leave a reply and she will get back to you in the fall.

Damn.

Sartre traveled like a pro and managed to stay nice and quiet while I smuggled her into Mongolia. She was a good sport. Now, I realize that sneaking a rodent into a foreign country isn't usually a good idea.

But this little pig went everywhere with me. She was kind of a security blanket. I wondered what the philosopher I named her after would think of that.

"*Sain bainuu!*" Sansar-Huu called out as he met me on the tarmac.

"*Sain ta sain bainuu?*" I replied with a hug.

"Fine, my friend!" he continued in English. "And how are your animals fattening up?"

I laughed at this traditional greeting and patted my sling holding Sartre. "Fattening up just fine." My pig squeaked in protest.

Sansar-Huu, whose name meant "Son of Cosmos," laughed as he took my duffel bag. After I shouldered my backpack, we walked across the tarmac to where a very beat-up Chevy truck stood waiting.

"What? No camels?" I teased.

Sansar-Huu proudly patted the rattletrap. "I just got this! My new truck!"

We climbed inside and began to make our way over the bumps and potholes that dotted the road. My friend was very proud of his newest acquisition, and I was happy for him. It always amazed me how two different cultures could call something "new" and it didn't at all mean the same thing. His truck was a far cry from what we would consider new in America. And yet he was just as excited about it. Vehicles were a rarity here in the countryside. To have anything with an engine was a big deal. Sansar-Huu was probably considered a wealthy man.

I sighed and relaxed. There was something very

peaceful about being in a place untouched by modern society. No cell phones ringing all over the place. No one on a laptop in a Starbucks—mainly because there was no Starbucks. People lived off the land. They ate what they grew. Life was straightforward. I often thought that these people knew something we didn't. Maybe the real nirvana is in places like these instead of a loaded-up spa in Malibu.

"Your friend is here. He brought his family to meet you," Sansar-Huu said with a smile.

"Chudruk is here?"

He nodded. "They set up camp near the stream. You did not tell me his father is Yalta. My family was very happy to meet him in person."

"My apologies, my friend. I didn't realize they would travel here to see me. I thought I would meet up with them along the way." That was more in keeping with the way Mongols think. Time is almost too abstract for them. Datebooks and planners are irrelevant here. You just go until you meet up with someone.

"It is all right. Your *ger* is ready." He grinned. "My wife set it up two days ago."

I leaned my head back against the yellowed glass of the truck. Good. I was tired. International flights always wore me out. I didn't want to get to our camp and have to spend more time setting up my tent. Sartre complained with a loud *wheek!* I pulled her out of the sling and held her on my lap.

"What is that?" my host asked.

"It's my pet guinea pig."

Sansar-Huu laughed loudly. Animals were treated differently here. Dogs were kept outside always, no matter what the weather, and they certainly never got up on the furniture. The people here ate everything else. I explained to Sansar-Huu that Sartre was my friend. He laughed even harder. Oh, well. You'd have culture clash sometimes. And as long as they didn't try to eat her, like some friends of mine in Peru tried to do two years ago, we'd be okay.

We entered the Bogd Khan Uul Strictly Protected Area, paid for our tickets into the park and drove on. The scenery was breathtaking—fragrant cedar trees beside crystal streams and verdant grasslands. I stared out the window as Sansar-Huu rambled on about the weather. Eventually we came over the crest of a small hill to see the valley below, framed in the shadows of sunset, filled with small white dots. Those dots were our tents, or *gers*. This was where I'd be living for the next few weeks.

I had met most of Sansar-Huu's family years ago. I'd kept in touch through letters. But his family had grown quite a bit in the last decade and a half. Sansar-Huu had told me he and his wife had five children. But I counted at least two dozen running around in the waning sunlight, laughing.

We pulled up about fifty yards from the first *ger*. A smiling woman with a weathered face and a thick, long braid came out and toward me, arms outstretched. This was Odgerel, Sansar-Huu's wife.

She began speaking in rapid Mongolian. I barely kept up. I think she said something about her goats being happy to see me, or the mare was too busy drinking alcohol to say hello. Apparently, my Mongolian was rustier than I thought.

I got settled in my *ger* and set up the small, collapsible cage I'd packed for Sartre, then made my way to Sansar-Huu's *ger* for dinner. My muscles ached from the bumpy drive and a full day of travel. I sat on the floor, enjoying the company while I ate sheep stew, then, after a few bowls of vodka, made my way back to my tent and bed. I don't even remember falling asleep.

"Coney! Coney Bombay!" The cry from the door woke me, and I staggered to my feet.

"Come in!" I shouted, quickly putting on clothes. Chudruk threw my door open and stepped inside with a smile. The years had been kind to him. Tall for his people, he was sinewy and strong. His name meant "fist." I never knew why.

Chudruk and I embraced, patting each other on the back. Within moments I had started a fire in the stove in the center of the room and was boiling water for tea. Mongolians prefer it with milk and salt. Sometimes they add animal fat. I was a real trooper about trying new things, except when it came to tea. I'd brought Earl Grey and a pound of sugar with me on this trip.

"Ahhh," Chudruk said as he drank deeply. "I do miss Western tea."

I tossed him a second box of Earl Grey and a large bag of sugar. "I brought you a little extra. I remember that sweet tooth of yours."

He nodded. "I'd never had sugar until I went to the States. It ruined me for this place." He stuck the tea and sugar in his jacket. "But that's okay. I'll survive somehow." He tossed me a felt bag.

"This is beautiful. Who knitted it?" The bag was a gray that graduated halfway down the bag into black. The felt was strong.

"My mother made it for you. For your training." He motioned to the opening. "Look!"

I pulled out an open-chested jerkin made of turquoise silk, a pair of purple silk underpants and a pair of leather boots, upturned at the toes. The embroidery on the boots and uniform was exquisite. Threads of silver and gold trailed and entwined impossibly across the surface of both garments.

"You have to train in this too." He pulled a pointed-topped cap from his jacket. "I almost forgot."

I shook my head. "I brought some training clothes."

Chudruk smiled. "I promised the guys I'd upload some photos of you in this on my Facebook page."

"Fantastic," I growled as I stripped, then put on the outfit. I felt like an idiot prancing around in what basically constituted a Speedo, two sleeves and pointy boots.

"I don't want to ruin them," I tried.

Chudruk waved me away as he tried to avoid doubling up with laughter. "No! You look great!" Hey! Where had he gotten that camera? "Say 'goat cheese'!"

I was still scowling as I stepped outside to find thirty-some Mongolians waiting for me. The women smiled and giggled. The men laughed with something I suspected was more mockery than anything else. Chudruk laughed and dragged me over to a man who appeared to be a shorter, older version of my friend.

"Coney," he began, "this is my father. Yalta."

My new coach nodded abruptly in my direction, and I returned the nod. Shaking hands wasn't a common activity here.

The crowd faded away. There was a lot of work to do before the day's end, and everyone was needed. I had given the two families a male and a female dairy cow and six goats each. The animals had been delivered just before I arrived. This would pay for my boarding and for the rudeness I'd be displaying by training and not helping out. These people never asked for it. But I wanted to thank them.

Yalta and Chudruk led me down to the stream, where my friend continued his introduction.

"My father does not speak English, so I will translate. He is the winner of three national *naadams*. He has the rank of bull. And he has agreed to train you."

"*Tand bayarlaa*," I thanked him. This was a big deal. A man like Yalta was as important in Mongolia as Joe Montana or Johnny Depp was in America.

"The first thing you have to do is fifty push-ups in

the stream." Chudruk translated his father's rapid-fire Mongolian.

"In the stream?" I asked, hoping he was kidding. The water in a creek like this came from melting snow in the mountains. It had to be about twelve degrees.

Yalta frowned and nodded. He seemed to take my question as an affront. I did as I was told and got in the water. My skin felt as if it was frozen hard, but I kept going until I had done fifty. As I got to my feet, I tried not to shiver. The two men were whispering as they watched me.

Yalta pointed to a large stone next to the stream.

"Pick it up," Chudruk translated. "Twenty-five over-head presses, please."

What could I do? I struggled to lift the stone. It was as wide as my shoulders and probably about seventy-five pounds. Still, I did what I was asked. My brief complaint earlier would no doubt turn on me later. I didn't want Yalta to think I couldn't handle the first five minutes of training. I still had a whole month to go.

Four hours later, bruised and exhausted, I slipped into my *ger*, ate a smuggled-in protein bar and chugged two cups of tea. Yalta had decided I was weak and needed rest. I didn't protest. I didn't even remove my uniform or boots—just buried myself under layers of wool blankets. I think I even fell asleep with my hat on.

I'd like to think it was jet lag, combined with my

pitiful training back in the States. I'd prefer to believe that, instead of the fact that I wasn't as young as I used to be. And that hurt. Still, I was completely and utterly useless. And tomorrow, I'd do it all over again.

Chapter Seven

Narrator: You can swallow a pint of blood before
   you get sick.

—*Fight Club*

"Wheeeeeeek!" Who needed a rooster when you had a
demanding guinea pig? I brought my arm up to move
the blankets and my muscles threatened to assassinate
me. The pig continued to protest, and I was worried
she would wake up the whole camp.

I managed to toss some fruit mixed with hay into
the cage and collapsed back onto my cot. It was dark,
and the stove had long since run out of fuel. There was
a chill in the air that was not helped by my skimpy
clothes. After lighting the kerosene lantern, I filled the
stove from a bucket of dried dung and lit a match. It
took only a few moments for the space to warm up.

The *ger* was basically a round tent covered in felted
wool. In the middle of the tent stood a small stove.
The pipe disappeared through a hole in the top. To
the left of the door I had my cot, two trunks for my
things, two stools and a rug. A box of cooking and
eating utensils stood next to the bucket of dried ma-
nure. This might be the first time in my life I was

happy to be the proud owner of a bucket of shit. A simple life, really.

I stood and started stretching to relieve my aching body. Fortunately, I had some life-giving ibuprofen in my backpack. I took three with the tea I'd warmed up on the cookstove. The heat flowed down my throat, and I started to feel a little like myself again. Wow. Hours of bizarre, sadistic exercises and wrestling one-on-one with a famous athlete. Maybe I wasn't doing so badly after all. And what time was it anyway, seven or eight at night?

A quick look at my watch made me do the traditional cartoon double take. Five a.m? How was that possible? I'd been sleeping since one o'clock in the afternoon!

Sartre paused in her eating to give me a disapproving, "Wheek." She sure told me.

I reached into my duffel to grab a fistful of protein bars. I was just reaching for my third when I felt something in there that I did not pack. That was weird. It felt like . . . like an envelope.

I pulled it out and dropped it onto my cot with a sigh. There was no mistaking the Bombay family seal. This was a job. But how in the hell did it find me all the way out here? I looked around for hidden cameras. I wouldn't be surprised to find photos of me in my flattering uniform in the family newsletter. Assassins are mean pranksters.

After throwing on a sweatshirt and jogging pants, I

carefully opened the door and slipped outside. Sansar-Huu's truck was rusting in the same spot where he'd parked it two days ago. There were no vehicle tracks in the long steppe grass. No hoofprints. Nothing. I circled the camp, then made my way back inside.

How did a Bombay manage to get this to me out here? And why now? I'd done two jobs in the last nine months. That was more than enough for a year. In fact, we usually had only one job a year. That was why I'd planned this trip. I figured my particular services weren't required.

The envelope was plain, the standard eight and a half by eleven inches. The only thing that identified it as a Bombay job was the bloodred wax seal stamped with the family crest. I set the envelope on my lap. Then I picked it back up. My curiosity was too great. And since I had no early morning cartoons or Pee Wee Herman cable reruns out here, I had to get my entertainment somewhere.

The only sounds coming from the camp were those of nature. No human was awake yet. I still had time. Very slowly, I broke the seal and slid open the envelope. The face of a European stared up at me. This was no Mongolian. How far would I have to go to get this done?

After reading the file, I put everything back in the envelope and shoved it to the bottom of my duffel to burn later. It was pretty cut-and-dried. My Vic was a Dutch mercenary named Arje Dekker. Usually I didn't mind mercenaries. In fact, sometimes they maintained the balance of civility in foreign countries rife with infighting and a weak military. This bastard, however, was different.

Selling out to the highest bidder, Dekker had no problem with who was paying him to do what. Interpol was investigating several accusations of extreme torture perpetrated by Dekker, mostly on women and children in a troubled African nation. This was one of the times I was grateful the Bombay Council didn't give me too much information.

Apparently Dekker was hiding out in none other than Mongolia. There were reports he was going to be at the national *naadam* in July in the capital. I was to use any means necessary to make him "disappear." And suddenly, I had no problem with mixing business with pleasure.

"You are supposed to throw him to the ground," Chudruk managed somehow amidst hysterical laughter. "He is an old man and you are young." He doubled over, trying to catch his breath.

I stood up and dusted off my shorts and T-shirt. It had taken twenty minutes, but I'd convinced Yalta to let me train in my own clothes. The *zodag* and *shuudag* were just too much, and I suspected I was wearing them merely to entertain my hosts. I kept the *gutals* on. Since this game was played on foot, I knew I had to break them in.

Yalta grinned and slapped his thighs, indicating that he was ready. I slapped mine in reply and we got to it. This time, I managed to keep him in a lock until he kicked my legs out from under me. In my mind, that was a victory.

We went through the same scenario no less than twelve more times, dammit. Still, I didn't complain and kept working. By late afternoon, I was covered in sweat, dust and bruises, while Yalta's *deel* sported nary a wrinkle. But that was good, right? I wanted a coach. A real *zazul* to help me. Not so I would win. There was no way I could go up against men who had been doing this since they were toddlers. I just wanted to experience it. And not embarrassing myself in the process was also good.

Why did I want to put myself through this? Well, why not? To me it was more of a question of what I didn't want out of life than what I did. I could have had a normal life as a college professor in some little town in New England. I'd spend my days lecturing countless kids on why the words of a guy who died three hundred years ago were important and relevant. Then I'd head home to grade papers, eat supper and watch TV or read until I fell asleep. If I were lucky, I might have a wife and kids to break the tedium. Eventually the college would force me to retire, and just maybe I would travel a little, or maybe I'd read books on my front porch until I died.

The truth was, after spending all those years studying philosophy, I realized that nothing written by Hobbes, Aquinas or Kant told me anything about life. Granted, I understood the idea that philosophy was the study of why we are here . . . the meaning of life and such. And yet it somehow wasn't. To me, these old dead guys felt that the only way to live your life was to sit and think of what it all meant. Then they died not even knowing if they were right. What the hell?

And then there was the part of me that was Bombay. I was born into a career I did not ask for. I was a hired killer. Try wrestling with the ideas of Mahatma Gandhi while learning how to fieldstrip a Remington sniper rifle. It just doesn't work. Well, there was that time I was stringing garrotes while listening to Niccolò Machiavelli's classic on tape, but that was an isolated incident.

Somewhere along the line, I became fascinated with the idea that while mankind aspired to apply thought and reason to life, they actually used violence to live it. Isn't that interesting? Not terribly deep, but it struck me as interesting. So, I took some serious martial-arts training on campus. This was about the time I was in love with a young woman named Frannie Smith, so I had other interests, like sex.

When Frannie dumped me right after graduation, I knew I would have to be a nomad. I rejected the very idea of having a normal life. That was how I ended up a carney. And that was when I started these little sabbaticals. Neat, huh? I'll bet you were expecting something else. Trust me, aside from being a knitting assassin/carney with a black belt in aikido and a proud guinea pig parent (I have the bumper sticker on my trailer), I'm not that complicated.

"You really gave us a show today," Sansar-Huu said as he and Chudruk sat down next to me on a rock beside the stream. They had hit it off immediately, so now I had two of them giving me a hard time.

"I aim to entertain." I pulled off my boots and stepped barefoot into the icy water. It felt wonderful. I felt alive. Battered but alive.

"Oh, you do, my friend," Sansar-Huu answered. "My wife wants to know if you will actually eat dinner tonight or if you are planning to insult us by going straight to bed again."

I wiggled my toes in the cold water, enjoying the shock. "I am sorry I offended you, my most gracious host." I wasn't being facetious. I really was sensitive to the fact that my nonappearance at dinner as a guest was noticed. You couldn't go to a country like this, where hospitality was an important part of life, and act like an arrogant American.

"I will be there and bring my appetite."

"Good," Chudruk said. "And be thirsty. I'm bringing *airag*."

"I can handle it." At least, I hoped I could. *Airag*, or *koumiss*, as it is sometimes called, is a potent alcoholic drink made of fermented mare's milk. I know, it doesn't sound tough, but the first time I drank it I lost my voice—and the lining of my esophagus—for a day and a half. And these men were serious drinkers. I would have to walk a fine line of drinking enough to make my hosts happy and not too much that I'd be in a coma in the morning.

"Just be ready," Chudruk said. "Yalta is going to start with the *mekhs.*"

There was a word I didn't know. "*Mekhs?*" I asked.

"It means . . ." He scratched his chin thoughtfully for a moment. There was no dictionary or Internet out here on the steppes. I hoped he could figure it out. The light came into his eyes and he smiled. "Techniques. My father is going to show you how to wrestle the way his father and grandfather taught him."

Stepping out of the stream onto the grass felt good. I toyed with washing up but decided against it. The sun was low in the sky and I wanted to make sure I changed before dinner in Sansar-Huu's *ger.*

The two men rose and started to walk away as I put my boots back on.

"By the way," I shouted. My stomach rumbled, and I realized I was very, very hungry. No PowerBars tonight. Tonight I was going fully native. "What are we eating?"

Sansar-Huu waved and shouted back, "Testicle soup!" As he turned away, I had the distinct feeling that he was smiling.

Chapter Eight

"Gravity is a harsh mistress."

—*The Tick*

The next few days went as you can imagine. I survived the testicle soup and found it really was not that bad . . . if you imagined it more like Campbell's chicken and dumplings, and had a lobotomy to rid your brain of the meaning of the word *testicle*. The mind works in mysterious ways.

As my training continued, I found, as I always did, that my stamina increased. So did my stubbornness. And slowly, very, very slowly, I started to understand what I needed to do. In my opinion, fighting was eighty percent mental. Every time I was thrown, I learned something. Granted, I wasn't as good as even the most amateur wrestler, but I was beginning to understand the physics of this form of wrestling. (Psst . . . it's all leverage.)

I asked Chudruk to forget the archery and horseback competitions (partly this was because I was afraid Sartre would see the horse as a compatriot in her mocking of me). It would take everything I had to get through the wrestling. And I had my first *naadam* in a couple of days. Trying to concentrate on two sports didn't make much sense. All of my faculties would be needed to stay upright and avoid as much humiliation as I could. I knew I would lose my first few competitions. But the longer I stayed on my feet, the more I would learn.

The *naadam* was a local competition lasting only one day. These were held throughout the country, with the crowning event being the national *naadam*, which was three days in mid-July. I wanted to prove myself, so I started training harder. Before Yalta made it to the stream where we worked, I was already there and had completed sixty, then seventy push-ups. I could lift larger stones over my head. I even managed to catch my *zazul* off guard, tripping him to where he landed on one knee. It counted. Anytime you caught your opponent off balance so that a hand, knee or back hit the ground, it counted. I didn't even gloat when I helped him up.

Of course, this also meant that I'd had a couple more evenings of *airag* and various questionable boiled sheep parts. But I didn't mind that anymore. Sansar-Huu's and Chudruk's families were becoming my family. And I didn't have to kill anyone to be part of it. That was very refreshing.

Everyone but a couple of teenagers traveled with me to the *naadam*. The smaller children promised to feed Sartre. They were fascinated with her. She was less so with them, but I threw in some fresh grass and she was in hog heaven.

Yalta had two grandsons in the competition besides

me. Apparently, they did not need him as much as I did, because it seemed to me I used up most of his time. Chudruk gave me a gift —a beautiful chocolate-colored *deel* made by his mother for my first competition. I was grateful and told her I would try even harder not to fall, in her honor. She thought this was very funny.

Sansar-Huu surprised me with my own peaked hat. It was black and square with a sort of steeple at the top. I thanked him, feeling a little overwhelmed by the generosity of these two families.

As we all piled into Sansar-Huu's truck, I wondered if I would see my vic, Dekker, at this *naadam*. I didn't expect to. My intel said only that he would appear at the national event. And it didn't say what he would be doing there. Would he just be a spectator, or a participant? If he was anything like me, I'd have guessed he was planning on wrestling too. He was a man of action. It would be unlike him to just sit and watch. On the other hand, he could just be curious or passing through. There really was no way of knowing why he was there, so I gave up trying.

The truck bumped along, jostling the riders in the back. I had tried to give up my passenger seat to Odgerel's mother, but everyone insisted I sit up front. I was their guest, they explained. If I had pressed the matter, they would've been insulted, so I did as I was told. If I didn't, I suspected we would have testicle soup every day for the rest of my visit.

My friend and guide pointed out the various wildlife along the way. There was so much life here. So much stark beauty. I felt at peace in this place. As I looked out the window, I tried to picture Genghis Khan and his men riding on their horses beside me as they made their way toward China or Russia, Persia or Europe, seeking conquest.

Genghis Khan was the reason for the *naadams*. He believed that wrestling, archery and horseback riding were the three manly games that tested his men's mettle for the battlefield. He was a sacred son here. And his nomadic ways were still revered by the very people in this truck.

We arrived at the site of the games two hours later. Men walked around in their wrestling uniforms or carried large bows. There were horses everywhere. A few *ger*s formed a circle in the grass, where, I was told, the wrestling games would take place. Yalta went to arrange for my competition as I removed my *deel* and donned my *zodag* and hat. As I warmed up, my thoughts went to my training. I imagined every possible action and reaction. My brain prepared to think without me. It had to be instinctive. My concentration was focused on the possibilities.

"You will wrestle seventh," Chudruk said to me quietly.

"Do you know who?" I asked, measuring up the other athletes. There was quite a range, from short, skinny guys to men who qualified for sumo wrestling. Yalta had explained that the matchups weren't based on fairness but randomness. So a neophyte like me could end up fighting a seasoned champion in my first match.

"Not yet. Does it matter?" my friend answered.

It did to me. I was kind of hoping to wrestle a four-year-old who'd had some cold medicine recently, but figured that was too much to ask. As to their laissez-faire attitude on matchups? That made sense. On the battlefield, you didn't have the opportunity to pick your opponent or the luck of having to fight someone weaker or the same size as you. Why should that tradition end now just for my comfort?

The very first match was actually between Yalta's grandson Zerleg and a favorite who had won many competitions and even qualified at the rank of *arslan*, or "lion." Zerleg was a tall, thin youth about seventeen years old. His name meant "savage," and he was anything but. From what he had told me one night, he wanted to be a poet. Wrestling was something he was doing for his grandfather's approval. Chudruk thought he had talent.

I watched as both young men did the *devekh*, or "eagle dance." They each stood at opposite ends of the circle, walking around their coaches, flapping their arms like eagles. It was a very graceful dance, an interesting introduction to a fighting competition.

Both men slapped their thighs, indicating their willingness to begin. I couldn't take my eyes off them. This was the first time I was seeing this tradition in person. The athletes walked slowly around each other, crouched and ready for grappling. In a split second,

Zerleg's opponent reached forward and the two men were locked, hands on each other's shoulders, each straining against the other's strength.

I'm always surprised when people watch matches like this, or Brazilian jujitsu, and think nothing is going on. Action has come to a standstill and the men seem to be holding still. Nothing could be further from the truth. Very small, very important movements are being made, like a chess game of the flesh. You may not be able to make it out, but the grapplers are inching their way, inflicting their will in millimeters of movement. And each flicker, each strain is a physical action that must be countered or one man will be thrown.

The men stand still for so long, sometimes I start to wonder if they've frozen this way.

"Sometimes the *bukh*s will stay this way for hours," Sansar-Huu whispered in my ear. "Sometimes a match can last all day. It usually isn't allowed at the national level, but sometimes here . . ." He shrugged.

I watched, transfixed, as Yalta called out to his grandson. It was obvious he was encouraging him, but I wasn't sure how. Would I understand what he was saying to me when it was my turn? I hadn't thought of that. I was quite familiar with the language, but if it wasn't for Chudruk translating for his father, I would still be doing push-ups in the stream.

The old men sitting on a blanket up front never blinked, as far as I could see. These were the judges, and whatever they said would be final. Their eyes squinted against the summer sun, missing nothing. I suspected they would do better than the controversial computer at the Olympic games.

On the grass, Zerleg and his opponent continued to strain. Sweat drizzled down the side of my face. It was about sixty-five degrees here, and yet I was perspiring in nothing more than briefs and an open-chested blouse. *Hmmm . . . maybe I should wear this when I work back home. Hello, ladies!*

Zerleg made an aggressive move: He slipped his right shoulder down to his opponent's hip and made a play to sweep him off his feet. I could feel my shoulders turning rock hard with tension. For a second, Zerleg seemed to have the advantage, as both of the other man's feet swung up off the ground. But with an amazing recovery, he managed to land flat-footed. Zerleg was so startled, he missed the fact that he was being shoved backward by the other guy's hands. He was on the ground, stunned, as the call was made that he had lost and would not be competing any further.

The opponent threw his arms up in the air and grandstanded for a moment. Zerleg reached up for assistance and the victor scoffed and walked away. I'd seen that look on the face of many a bully over my lifetime (and, fortunately, I'd been able to kill a few of them). Yalta helped his grandson up and patted him on the back as they walked off the playing field. The boy looked miserable, but as his grandfather and coach kept whispering in his ear, he finally broke into a sad smile. This was his first match. He did very well.

I joined in congratulating him, and his spirits seemed to rise. Although I don't think that was as much because of me and his family as because of the cluster of giggling teenage girls waving at him from across the field. Within moments he had put on his *deel* and was walking over to them. I had to smile. He might have lost the game, but his poetry would likely score him some points today.

The other matches were equally as tense and no less dramatic. By the time the fourth contest ended, I realized I needed to take my eyes off the field and focus on my own upcoming competition. I sat down on a blanket with Sansar-Huu's wife, Odgerel, and closed my eyes. My thoughts were devoted exclusively to all that I had seen today and what Yalta had taught me. The sounds around me were tuned out until it was just me picturing how it would or could go down.

"Coney!" Chudruk shook me. "It is your turn." He led me to the field to where my *zazul*, Yalta, stood quietly. I turned only to see who my competitor was. It was the bully who'd defeated Zerleg. As I began my eagle dance, I pictured what I had seen him do before. He was my size and weight. We would be more evenly matched than he was with the boy. But this man had experience I didn't.

My dance ended, I crossed the field to my opponent and slapped my thighs. He grinned and did the same. Our contest had begun.

I had decided that I wouldn't walk around him but would immediately make the first move, which I did, grabbing him by the shoulders. He gripped mine with hands that felt like steel, matching my strength. Jesus. What did they feed these guys? Was it the soup?

We strained against each other, our heads looking down at our legs for an opening . . . a sign of weakness. Sweat made it difficult to hold on, but I didn't give in. My fingers and arms burned, but I knew that if I eased up the slightest bit, it would all be over. And that was when I knew that this was going to be much harder than I ever imagined.

And I had thought this was a good idea . . . why?

Chapter Nine

Luther: Warriors, come out to play-ay.

—*THE WARRIORS*

I gritted my teeth, which hurt, by the way. It felt like I was going up against a steel beam, which also seemed silly. Now I understood why my training involved wrestling with boulders. This was damn near the same thing.

My opponent kicked at my feet, hoping to knock me down. I looped my right leg around his right leg and tried to trip him. He didn't budge. It was like trying to topple a redwood tree. I got my feet planted before he could take advantage of my being off balance. We continued to strain.

At some point, it became clear that we could very well be like this all day. He had the best of me and knew it, but I refused to budge . . . a typical Bombay trait. Soon, however, I would have to break. My muscles weren't trained for this kind of torture and were rudely beginning to complain.

I've been told that because of my pale blue eyes, I have an unnerving gaze. Maybe that would work against an opponent who only ever saw brown eyes grimacing back at him. It was crazy and a little stupid, because my concentration would shift. But it seemed like a good idea at the time.

I looked up and stared at the top of his head. What was I thinking? He wouldn't look up. Why would he? I continued to stare at his sweat-soaked dark hair as I held him off at the shoulders. The longer I did, the more I realized that only he could see the position of our legs and feet, giving him the advantage. But I didn't look down. *Look at me, damn you!* I thought over and over.

By some small miracle, he actually looked up! I was about to wonder if I was telepathic but abandoned that idea, directing every ounce of energy that wasn't shoving against this brick wall into my glare. Our eyes locked just like our bodies. Great. So much for that idea.

Until I felt him give a little bit. Not more than a slight shift in his elbow, perhaps. I stared as hard as I could, even though it felt a little ridiculous. The stress was unimaginable. I've never, in any fight, had an opponent who didn't budge in any way. Even his flesh was hard. I decided it was time to use something that had worked for me on other objects of prey. I winked at him.

His eyes widened slightly, and I felt a fleeting slip of victory. Without looking down, I moved my left leg around his and shoved with every ounce of strength I had left. I felt his stance shift. His shoulders gave slightly. I had him! In just a second, he'd be down on the ground and Zerleg would sort of be avenged.

I knew the second I did it that taking my eyes off him was a mistake. But something glinted in the distance, just behind his ear. There was no stopping my wandering eyes as I found the source of my distraction. Blonde hair. There was a woman with blonde hair standing there, her eyes wide and her mouth shaped like an O. I couldn't stop myself. It was too late, and as my opponent took advantage of my breaking concentration and I fell backward to the ground, the very surprised face of Veronica Gale watched.

I never took my eyes off of her as I rose to my feet and walked over to my coach.

"You did really well." Chudruk clapped me on the back. Yalta nodded.

"Thanks." I knew I had done well. It didn't make me feel better. I wanted to beat that smarmy son of a bitch, but my guard had been lowered and he kicked my ass.

"No, really!" Sansar-Huu laughed. "You lasted longer than anyone else has. Not bad for your first match."

I turned toward my friends. They were complimenting me. I needed to cool down. No one expected me to win. This was my first *naadam*. In their minds, the fact I'd lasted so long was cause for celebration.

"*Tand bayarlaa,*" I said with more feeling this time. And I meant it. Cooling my heels was a good idea, because I was pretty sure that if I spoke to Miss Gale now, I'd explode.

We walked back to the others and they all joined in the congratulations. I only half listened as Zerleg in particular grinningly told the story in more detail than I remembered. Apparently, he was satisfied that I'd avenged his loss. At least that was something.

My brain buzzed. What the hell was Ronnie doing here? This was no mirage. I saw her. And what were the odds she'd be in Mongolia . . . let alone this tiny fragment of it? I wanted answers to these questions, but not yet. First I had to honor my friends, who'd done so much to get me this far.

"To Coney!" Chudruk pushed a glass of vodka into my hands and raised a toast. Both families cheered as I drained my cup. The warmth surged through my veins, which was good, because I was still wearing my uniform and it was a bit chilly.

"Cy?" Veronica's voice caught me off guard, and I turned to see her at the edge of the crowd. The Mongolians stared at her. I wondered if any of them had ever seen a blonde woman before.

I nodded to my hosts, then crossed over to her. She looked me up and down, then did something unexpected. Veronica Gale burst into laughter.

"You . . . you look great!" She giggled.

"What the hell are you doing here?" I growled.

This drew her up short. "You . . . you're mad at me?"

I wrestled mentally with this one. "No," I lied.

She pointed at me, eyes wide in astonishment. "You *are* mad at me! Unbelievable!"

"I'm not mad at you," I said quietly, clearly indicating that I was. "I'm just upset at losing my concentration and losing the match."

Her eyes narrowed and she put her hands on her hips. "You blame me for this! Don't you?"

I took her by the elbow and guided her away from the others. "No. I don't blame you for this." Because that would be unreasonable. "I blame myself." *Liar.*

Veronica did not look convinced. "Right."

We stared at each other for an uncomfortable moment. Then I realized I was actually happy to see her, in spite of being pissed off.

"Let's take a walk," I said as I took her hand and led her away from the festival. We didn't have to go very far to find a place to be alone. We must have looked odd to the Mongolians—two blond Caucasians, bickering. Veronica just held on to my hand and followed.

It surprised me how intimate it felt to hold her hand. I didn't have many opportunities for that. Most of my liaisons since college didn't feature enough time for that simple, affectionate act. Holding Ronnie's hand made me feel the stirrings of an emotion I'd long since given up on.

There was a collection of rocks about two hundred yards from the party. I sat down on a large, flat stone and Veronica joined me, dropping my hand and drawing her knees up under her chin. It was pretty adorable.

"What are you doing here?" The walk had given me a chance to calm down.

"I could ask you the same thing." She met my gaze defiantly. It seemed as though, while my anger had dissipated, hers was just heating up.

"I'm here to participate in the festival."

"I'm here to observe it," she said flatly. I guess she was pissed off with the way I'd acted.

"Why?"

"It's part of my doctoral thesis. And I'll be interviewing natives and outsiders at the national competition. I came early to get a grasp on everything." Veronica looked away for a moment, as if she didn't want to meet my eyes.

"Another paper, eh?" I grinned.

"I take my education very seriously."

"I believe that. But what will you do once there is nothing left to study?"

Her shoulders slumped, and I wished I could've taken the words back. "I don't know."

I decided to change tack. No point in beating her up over this. I'd done it enough before.

"So, tell me how coming here relates to your thesis," I said with what I hoped looked like a reassuring smile as I sat there on a rock in pink briefs.

"My dissertation examines the ways men choose to glorify violence through everything from tribal war games to murder and assassination. Unfortunately, my thesis committee considered my writing 'too stiff and dry,' so they wanted me to observe these war games up close and hopefully apply that to my research."

"But the national *naadam* isn't for another few weeks," I pointed out. "Why come early?"

"My professors thought it would be good for me." She cocked her head. "Do I seem dull to you?"

I laughed. "No. Not at all. I had fun with you in Miami." And I did too, I realized.

"Well, the people I work with think I don't know how to live. They believe I think *fun* is a four-letter word."

My laughter came a little harder. "At least you didn't correct them there."

Her eyes grew wide. "What do you mean by that? Of course I told them *fun* has three letters."

Wow. She needed to lighten up. "You know what? I understand why they sent you here now."

She fairly growled. "Well, I don't get it. Honestly— Mongolia? Why couldn't I find something like that in Paris? But no, I have to pick something located in a barren wasteland where the language is impossible. Fine. I'm here, but I don't have to like it."

I couldn't help smiling. Was I the only person who found this little tiff engaging?

"I mean," Veronica continued, "who in their right mind thinks of Mongolia when going on her first vacation since starting college seven years ago? Well, it's too late to back out. It was nice of Professor Bialsky to arrange for a grant and everything, since I couldn't afford the trip otherwise. But why do I have the feeling in the back of my mind that they are trying to get rid of me?"

"Are you talking to me or yourself?" I asked.

"You are laughing at me."

"Only on the inside, I swear."

"Yeah, well, you wouldn't be laughing so hard if you had a mirror." With that she folded her arms.

I looked down at myself. My body was in peak condition. It wasn't terribly embarrassing to be wearing such a skimpy uniform.

"I mean, what's with the little panties and tiny shrug?" She started smiling at last. "And the little pointed hat and curly-toed boots? I can't figure it out!"

"All right, Ronnie. Here's your first lesson." I then explained the reason for the open-chested *zodag* and the fact that the "panties" were for ease of movement.

Unfortunately, I had no idea about the little hat and elflike boots.

Her mouth dropped open, and for a moment I wondered what it would be like to kiss that mouth when she was sober.

"You mean this . . . whatever you called it"—she fingered the edge of my sleeve—"is to keep women from competing? Seriously?"

I nodded. "Genghis Khan referred to this as the Three Manly Games. He used them not only to train his warriors, but also to pit political rivals against one another. He obviously believed the sport shouldn't be tainted by women. And the Mongolians concur."

She snorted. "Sounds mighty sexist to me."

I shook my head. "Genghis Khan wasn't exactly a feminist, but he had high regard for women. He revered his mother and his favorite wife. They had a lot of power for women of that time. But he felt that this was a man's world and sport."

"You sound like you admire him."

"I do. The man came from nothing. He was a peasant and a bastard, and ended up ruling an area stretching from Russia to China to India. He did this with a group of archers on horseback. He opened up the Silk Road, introducing East to West, and his sons and grandsons ruled Russia, China and India until the nineteen twenties. There's a lot to admire about a man like that."

Veronica sat silently, digesting the information. As a cultural anthropologist, she was bound to be interested.

"I read an article before I came," she said as she stared off into the distance, "that said that a large percentage of people in the world can trace their DNA back to Mongolia. That must be why."

I let her think for a while, soaking up her interest with affection. I loved learning. I missed the ivory tower a bit. Watching her think was somewhat erotic for me.

"I have an idea," I said after a while. "Why don't you come with us? Stay with me and my friends. You'll experience the culture and observe the training. And in my downtime, I can try to give you some insight into the . . ." I paused. "How did you put it? Violent interests of men?"

"Oh." She looked uncertain. "I don't know. . . ."

"Where are you staying now?" I asked.

"In Ulaanbaatar." She pointed to a rickety truck that made Sansar-Huu's beat-up Chevy look like a Rolls-Royce. "The driver brought me out here just for the day."

"I can't think of a better way for you to do what your committee wanted you to do than by joining us. And instead of feeling completely alienated back at the HoJo or whatever, you can learn about these people and their nomadic culture and have a built-in translator."

She considered this for a moment, much to my delight. I wanted her to stay. Wanted to be with her. Veronica Gale brought out something in me that had been dormant a long, long time. And I knew I could help her. And maybe there would be sex. I liked sex.

"But my things are in the hotel room," she protested weakly.

"I'll see if my friends can pick them up."

We sat for a moment, looking at each other.

"Okay," she replied, and I felt a wave of relief. "I'll do it."

I stood and took her hand, hauling her to her feet. "Let's go take care of the details. And then your education begins."

Chapter Ten

Villager: If he's the best with the gun and the knife,
   with whom does he compete?
Chris: Himself.

—*The Magnificent Seven*

Sansar-Huu immediately volunteered to let Ronnie
stay with his family. I was a little surprised until I remembered that the Mongols are famous for their hospitality. Veronica became somewhat shy around them.
She was definitely out of her comfort zone. Odgerel
patted a spot beside her on the blanket, indicating
that Ronnie should join her. I nodded in encouragement. With one last look up at me, Ronnie sat down
and was immediately handed vodka. She sipped it
carefully and smiled when she recognized it. Oh, this
was going to be fun. I couldn't wait for the family to
slaughter a sheep and divvy up the carcass for us to
eat right there on the floor.

Zolbin, Yalta's other grandson, had done quite well
and was in the finals. Part of his success was luck.
He had managed to draw competitors much smaller
than he was. Tall like his brother, Zolbin was heavier,
hewn with a great deal of muscle. He was much more
outgoing than his sibling and took to wrestling very

naturally. I was curious to see him go up against an athlete closer to his level.

I'd managed to get into my sweatpants and *deel*. Sitting in my uniform felt awkward. Others did it, but I wasn't them. And it took the comedic wind out of Ronnie's sails. When Zolbin was called up to wrestle, she joined me in front, slipping her hand into mine. I looked at her more closely as she observed the field. Her short hair blew in the wind. She wore a T-shirt and sweater with jeans and hiking boots. Watching the curiosity on her face inspired me. I remembered when I couldn't wait to learn everything and anything.

Zolbin was going through the motions of his eagle dance, and I noticed with surprise that his competitor was none other than the man who had bested me and Zerleg. This was going to get interesting.

"His name is Sukhbaatar." Chudruk appeared at my side. "It means 'Ax Hero.'"

Veronica looked at my friend with interest. "That's a tough name."

He nodded. "He is favored to do well at nationals."

The combatants slapped their thighs and we turned our attention to the field. Both men were matched for height and weight. The only difference was experience, as Chudruk whispered. Zolbin was a bit newer to the sport.

Unlike his cautious brother, Zolbin dove immediately for Sukhbaatar's hips. His opponent broke free and grabbed Zolbin's ankle. Zolbin spun on his heel and slipped from his grasp. Apparently, this match was going to be quite different. Sukhbaatar had to fight for every inch, and it became clear immediately that Zolbin's very aggressive and active fighting style was a problem for him. I noticed Zerleg cheering for his brother on the other side of Chudruk.

Sukhbaatar charged Zolbin's hips, but Zolbin stepped just out of reach. He spun behind Sukhbaatar and from behind managed to throw him to the ground. The crowd roared, and I noticed with some pleasure that Zerleg was pumping his fist in the air in celebration. Yalta even sported a slight grin.

Zolbin did not grandstand. He merely nodded modestly at the crowd, then walked over to his opponent, extending his hand. Sukhbaatar's face was bright red as he slapped Zolbin's hand away. The crowd jeered. No one, no matter what culture, thought bad sportsmanship was acceptable.

The families celebrated the win with cooked mutton bought from a vendor. More vodka was passed around, and we all got pleasantly drunk as the day drew to a close and the competition ended. By besting his opponent, Zolbin achieved the coveted rank of *zaan*, or elephant. Both families, Sansar-Huu's and Chudruk's, celebrated the win as if they were all related. This was the way of the steppes. They now had a connection, and I was more than a little touched that I was the catalyst.

I insisted that Yalta and Zolbin ride in the cab of the truck while Veronica and I climbed into the back with the others. The darkening sky brought a chill to the windy road as we drove along. I was warm in my fur-lined *deel*, but Ronnie began to shiver. I put my arm around her and pulled her close. She resisted at first, then relaxed against me. The alcohol buzzed warmly in my veins and I felt good.

Our friends chattered around us and I translated a bit for Ronnie. She laughed at the jokes a few moments later than they were told—and at many mangled translations I attempted—but I could tell she was starting to feel comfortable. That convinced me I had been right to invite her. In the sterile environment of a hotel in the big city, she wouldn't learn anything.

Eventually we arrived at the camp. Ogderel invited Ronnie to share their *ger*, but I insisted she be put up in mine. Too much cultural overload was not a good thing. It would be better if she was with someone she knew. Someone who spoke English. Someone who wanted to have sex with her. Yalta sent the boys over with an extra cot and blankets. Ronnie watched nervously as I set her up on the other side of the tent.

She sat quietly on her cot, cuddling Sartre while I made some tea. It was warm in the *ger*. The felt walls kept in the heat put out by the small cookstove.

"What are you doing?" she asked sharply.

I kept unbuttoning my *deel*. "Getting undressed."

Ronnie's face had a look of sheer panic. "Surely you aren't going to strip right here in front of me!"

"You've seen me in nothing but a towel. Get over it."

"I'll . . . I'll go outside and wait."

"Why?" I asked, even though I knew the answer.

"Can't you just sleep in that?" Patches of red spread over her cheeks.

I shook my head. "It chafes and isn't very warm." I found it hilarious that, in spite of her modesty, she didn't look away as I peeled off my *zodag*, leaving nothing but my *shuudag*. In fact, she looked a little frozen with fear.

"Well, since you can't take your eyes off of me, I'll turn around." I smiled. With my back to her, I pulled off the briefs, leaving myself completely naked. For a moment I entertained the thought of turning around . . . just for the fun of it. But the fact that she was nervous about being here changed my mind.

Did I imagine it, or was there a brief intake of air coming from this modest young lady? I slipped on a sweat suit and socks and turned around.

Veronica looked stricken. And maybe a little excited. I couldn't tell. It made me wonder if she had sex very often. Now, why did that pop into my head?

She accepted the tea gratefully and drank. "This is good. I was afraid you would give me more vodka. Or . . . what did they call it?"

"*Arikh.* You'll only see that in the cities and at festivals. For the most part, we will be drinking *airag*."

"What's that?"

"Fermented mare's milk."

She blanched. "Thank God you have tea."

"And that's another thing I should warn you about. They drink their tea with salt and animal fat." I watched with amusement as she grimaced. "But I have the good stuff."

She shook her head. "I never thought I'd hear tea called 'the good stuff.'"

I smiled. "There's a lot you will have to get used to here. We eat a lot of mutton and goat cheese. Just remember to stay away from *tarvag*."

"Why?"

"It's marmot. And they still carry the black plague."

Ronnie's eyes widened. "I guess I really am immersed in Mongolian culture now. What do we do during the day?"

"We aren't expected to help out, but I think you should. It will give you a little more experience. And Odgerel speaks some English. I'll be training. You are always welcome to watch Yalta kick my ass."

This made her smile. "I'd like that."

I nodded. "I knew you would." Exhaustion pulled at me, begging me to sleep. Veronica put the guinea pig back in her cage and slid between the blankets on her cot. I turned out the lantern.

"Good night, Ronnie," I said quietly as I climbed into my bed.

"Cy?" she replied in the darkness. "Thank you for

bringing me here, and for explaining and translating and everything."

"You are very welcome." And I meant it. Veronica Gale was getting under my skin, and I enjoyed it. In fact, I wondered, as I heard her breathe across the *ger*, whether I would actually get any sleep at all.

Chapter Eleven

"Those who are easily shocked should be shocked more often."

—MAE WEST

I decided to let Ronnie sleep in. She looked so comfortable snuggled beneath the wool blankets. Actually, I wanted to get in there with her warm, sleeping body. Wrap myself around her soft flesh . . .

Shaking my head to clear it, I shrugged on the rest of my clothes and, after chugging some tea and eating a couple of protein bars, went outside to meet Yalta at the stream.

"Pop says you did real good yesterday," Chudruk said with a grin.

"I could've done better," I replied.

He nodded. "Yes, you could have. But you were distracted."

I could feel my face warming in the cool morning breeze. Was I actually blushing? I didn't think I had it in me.

Yalta put his hand on my shoulder. He looked me in the eyes and spoke slowly so I would understand. Yeah, that made me feel better.

"You are good. You will do well at the *Naadam*

Festival," was all he said. At least, that was how I interpreted him. For all I know he called me an idiot unworthy of castrating sheep.

"*Tand bayarlaa*," I thanked him, but wasn't so sure I deserved the praise.

We trained for a few hours. This time, Yalta stressed technique more than strength training. I felt honored. He was showing me that I'd gone beyond his expectations. I was a Westerner who had made a good showing at the local *naadam*. We had another one in a few days, and Yalta told me he thought I could win at least one match.

I worked very hard. His faith in me was a great honor, and I wanted him to understand that I knew that. This was what I came here for: to test myself and learn. Maybe I wasn't too different from Veronica after all.

As we made our way back to camp at midday, I noticed that my fair and lovely roommate was sitting on the grass with Odgerel, making cheese. The Mongolian was speaking English slowly, and Ronnie seemed to understand.

"There is your man now." Odgerel pointed at me with a smile.

Veronica blushed a bright scarlet. "Oh! Um, he's not . . . Well, we're not . . ." She stumbled, at a loss for how to explain our situation.

"*Sain bainuu!*" I greeted the women, plopping down in the grass next to Ronnie. It was then that I noticed she had Sartre with her. The gluttonous pig was between the women, chowing down on the cool, damp grass.

"I hope you don't mind that I brought her out here. . . ." Veronica bit her lip.

I scooped up the pig. "Not at all. And you had her between you so the falcons wouldn't get her."

She nodded. "I was worried about that."

Sartre squealed, struggling to get out of my grip and back to the juicy grasses. I returned her to her place between the women and she regally ignored me.

I stood. "I'd better get back to the *ger*. I want to have some tea during my break."

Veronica looked at her hostess, then looked at me. She nodded and I took it to mean she was okay with that idea. Once in the tent, I stripped off the sweat-soaked shirt and replaced it with a dry one. After creating a fire on the stove and setting the kettle on, I lay on my cot to await the kettle's whistle.

Every inch of my body ached. And I was extremely proud of that. Being here and working toward my goal gave me a sense of peace. Funny, isn't it, how training for violence can make one feel that way? I stretched my legs out, kicking something with my foot. Odd. Everything should have been stowed in the trunks.

I sat up and saw that there was a suitcase with wheels and a briefcase sitting next to my bed. Must have been Ronnie's. Sansar-Huu made good on his promise and brought back her things from the city. I chuckled, thinking of Veronica trying to roll a suitcase on the steppes. My laughter came harder when I thought of her trying to plug in her laptop.

"Is something funny?" The source of my amusement entered the *ger*. She was smiling. I loved it when she smiled.

"Sorry. I just noticed you got your things." I pointed at the cases on the floor.

She rushed forward. "Oh! That's great!" I watched as she opened the case and began sifting through it. I was hoping she might pull out a slinky negligee or thong. But not Veronica. All of her clothes were plain and practical.

"I guess I won't need my laptop." She frowned as she held the plug.

"Paper and pen will have to do."

"I brought some, but not much." She pulled four large notepads out of her bag, and I wondered what she considered a lot.

"How much do you actually need?"

Veronica sat on the bed, looking thoughtfully at the hole in the roof where the stovepipe went. "I need to make notes, and I have to do that interview. . . ." She pulled a digital recorder out and checked the batteries.

I leaned back on the cot and closed my eyes. "If you need any help from me, I'll be right here."

There was no response.

The next two days were a blur of training. I noticed Ronnie watching me a couple of times but tried not to let her distract me. Most of the time I made it back to the *ger* I passed out before she showed up. This bothered me because I wanted to enjoy my time with her. And that bothered me because I was supposed to be focusing on training. Sartre spent most of her time in Veronica's pocket. I woke up at one point to find her sleeping next to my neck, but that was the most attention I got from her.

The day of the *naadam*, I found my uniform washed and waiting on my trunk. I wasn't sure whom to thank for that. After wrestling myself into it and putting on sweatpants and my *deel*, I headed outside to find everyone in the truck, waiting for me.

Veronica patted the front seat in the truck next to her. Yalta's grandsons sat in the back with him and the rest of the family. Sansar-Huu was driving. I spent the trip chewing on protein bars while my friend told my alleged girlfriend about the scenery. My thoughts drifted to my training and the techniques Yalta had taught me in the last few days. I was so focused, I almost missed the conversation going on next to me.

"Cy was so drunk, we found him out in the fields, curled up and sleeping with two goats."

Veronica laughed and looked at me. "You have interesting taste in females."

"Well, I do find you attractive," I replied, watching as her face reddened. "And that wasn't my fault. It was my first time with *airag* and this bastard told me it wasn't potent."

Sansar-Huu nodded. "It was interesting how those two goats followed you around for days afterward."

I remembered that. Coney's concubines, they called them at the time. Nice.

"I take it you don't date much?" Veronica asked with a little too much interest.

Chudruk chose that moment to pop his head through the little windows to the back of the truck. "You should see his little black book!"

I made a mental note to exact my revenge later.

"What little black book?" Ronnie's eyes grew wide. Surely she wasn't that naive.

Chudruk was practically bursting. "Oh, you know, the groupies. Cy has them in almost every city we hit."

My gut twisted at the reminder. I was hoping Veronica wouldn't ask about that.

"You brought that up when I interviewed you," she started. I couldn't decipher the look in her eyes. "Something about women with carney fantasies?"

This time, all three faces stared at me. I read amusement in Sansar-Huu's and Chudruk's faces. But Ronnie's features had darkened. I wrestled with how much to tell her.

"Come on, spill it," she said unconvincingly. "It's for my research." She didn't look like she really wanted to know.

Chudruk settled himself in the window. He wasn't going anywhere, which would make lying impossible. I sighed. There was no way out of this.

"There are some women who have a carney fetish." That was simple. Maybe I could stop there. I looked around so I could distract everyone by shouting, "Hey, there's a yak," or, "Is that Genghis Khan?"

"And?" Ronnie asked, biting her lip.

"It's usually bored, wealthy housewives. Something about having sex with a carney turns them on," I started slowly. She continued to stare. Okay. Fine. I went on. "I have a few women in some of the places we go who make sure I call them when I'm in town."

"And you have sex with them?"

"Yes."

Veronica looked like she wanted to punch me. "So you're a slut."

I shook my head. "No, I just have a casual sex life."

"Why sleep with them? They are using you!"

She was going from zero to volcanic in five seconds. "Don't take it personally, Veronica."

Chudruk decided this was the time to intervene. "Cy is the most popular. He has all of his teeth and is very clean."

Oh, yeah, that helped.

"You have the perfect life, my friend." Sansar-Huu sighed, not helping at all.

"It's no big deal," I started to explain. "I only hit most of those towns once a year. And it's not like I do it for money or anything."

"But they are using you!" she repeated.

I shook my head. "I don't see how. Seems to me I benefit from it as well."

If we weren't in such tight quarters, she might have put her hands on her hips. "And how do you do that? You are just a hollow figurehead . . . an object of desire to them."

"I fail to see what is wrong with that," I answered honestly. "I have no attachments in my life, and Sartre doesn't seem to mind. Why can't I have sex with anyone I want to?"

"What . . . what about diseases?" she sputtered.

"Believe me, these women take care of their bodies. And I always use protection." I was starting to get a little annoyed by her anger. This was my life, wasn't it?

Veronica folded her arms across her chest and stared straight forward.

Chudruk, on the other hand, didn't shut up. "Do you still see that one blonde from California? Man, she is so hot."

I turned to him. "You mean Katya?" I was pissed off by Ronnie's holier-than-thou attitude. "Yup. Saw her last year. She's very flexible."

Ronnie practically screamed, "You are such a poodle!"

This caught me off guard. I've been called many things in my life, from a greasy goon to a coldhearted killer. But this was new.

"She just keeps you in her purse! On a leash!" Veronica was losing it.

I shook my head. "Not Katya."

"Oh, and she's special, huh?" Ronnie snorted.

"No. She's just lonely. Her husband is an orthopedic surgeon who bought her online as a mail-order bride from the Ukraine. She has a master's degree in engineering, but no options at home, so she hooked up with a doctor and thought she could have a professional life in the United States."

Veronica was very silent.

"Unfortunately, her new husband is extremely possessive. Her bodyguards are like prison guards. Katya isn't allowed to have a job or work."

"But that's illegal!"

"You'd think so, wouldn't you? But he'll divorce her if she protests, and her citizenship could be revoked. She'd be right back where she started, in a Soviet-style crumbling apartment block, sharing her apartment with a family of eight."

Ronnie's anger had turned into interest. "How can you see her, then?"

"She takes her niece and nephew to the circus. Her sister-in-law picks them up there, she dodges the bodyguards and I usually find her in my trailer."

Chudruk slid the window shut and Sansar-Huu seemed overly fascinated with his steering wheel.

"So, without you, she'd be nothing more than a prisoner in a gilded cage," Veronica said slowly.

"Don't feel that it's all like that. She's the exception. The rest are just hot lays."

I could see her anger rising again. "Why would you tell me that?" she asked.

"Because for one thing, this is helpful to your research. And for another thing, I didn't want you to get the wrong idea about me." I grinned.

Needless to say, the rest of the ride was very, very quiet.

Chapter Twelve

"I am the punishment of God.... If you had not committed great sins, God would not have sent a punishment like me upon you."

—GENGHIS KHAN

Veronica ran off with Odgerel as soon as we parked the truck. Sansar-Huu walked with me to the fighting ring.

"Why did you tell her that last part?" he asked me.

"What?"

"Why did you tell her that most of the time you are just having sex for fun?"

"Because it is none of her business what I did in the past. And I didn't like being judged."

My friend nodded. "You are right, but you have a lot to learn about women." I watched him as he walked away, knowing he was right. But it pissed me off that Veronica, who was supposed to be objective in her studies, would be so angry with the way I'd lived my life so far. This was the main reason I stayed away from attachment in the first place. And here I was, getting involved again.

I didn't owe Ronnie anything. I was just an oddity she examined and judged . . . a footnote in a thesis.

Actually, I was starting to get angry with myself for the feelings I had for this woman. What had I been thinking? That I could change her? Loosen her up? What an idiot!

Focusing on the competition was my main concern. That was why I was here. Right? I took off my *deel* and pants and started warming up. Yalta, Zerleg and Zolbin joined me. All three of our matches were in a few hours. We concentrated on watching the games, taking note of the other athletes and their weak spots. I was determined to forget about Veronica.

I was so wrapped up in the contest that I barely made it to do the eagle dance for my own match. Clearing my head as I moved around Yalta, I ran through everything that could happen and how I would counter it. I slapped my thighs and made my way into the ring, squaring off against my opponent.

This time I didn't look him in the eyes. That barely worked last time. I wanted to try ignoring his face and concentrating exclusively on his movements. In fact, this strategy worked so well I had him on his back inside of a minute.

"Great job," my opponent growled in English at my feet.

I offered my hand to help him up. He grabbed it and pulled himself to his feet. My competitor wasn't Mongolian. Instead, I was staring into the face of Arje Dekker . . . my assignment.

"Don't see many Europeans here," he said as his eyes crinkled into a smile.

"I'm American," I said smoothly, hiding my shock behind a warm grin.

"Well, you kicked my ass," Arje answered. "Hopefully, I can regain my dignity later."

"Good luck with that," I said as I started to turn away.

He didn't answer, just chuckled as I walked toward my coach. I was in shock. Even though I knew my vic was in Mongolia, I didn't think I'd see him until the national event. It never occurred to me that he would be here doing what I was doing.

Yalta and the boys clapped me on the back, and Chudruk joined us.

"You followed his technique!" Chudruk noted. "Yalta is very happy with you."

I nodded and tried to turn my attention back to the competition. In a few hours I would have to fight again. My brain was a hot mess, between Veronica and Dekker. Focus was looking like a pipe dream at that point.

Zerleg lost his match, but narrowly enough that his grandfather was very proud. Zolbin defeated his opponent easily, and I was once again starting to get caught up in the festive atmosphere. The *naadam* was going well for us. Too bad my professional and personal life sucked.

This was too much. I understood the idea of coincidence. But to have both Veronica and Dekker here? Maybe something else was going on. In the Bombay family, you knew that just about anything was possible. After all, I never did figure out how they got the assignment to me.

I pulled on my *deel* and joined the others, who were having tea about one hundred yards from the ring.

"Where's Veronica?" I asked Odgerel. I don't know why. I didn't particularly want to speak to her.

Sansar-Huu's wife pointed over her shoulder, and I looked but couldn't see her. I stood chugging the hot tea and then wandered in that direction. Imagine my surprise when I spotted her talking to, of all people, Dekker. They seemed to be deep in conversation. This was bad. Dodging behind a *ger* (and feeling like an idiot for doing so), I tried to sort this out.

It made some sense to think they would spot each other. Caucasians tended to stand out here. If Veronica asked what he was doing at the competition, she'd have another guy like me to interview.

I peeked around the edge of the tent and saw that they were smiling. Damn. What if Dekker was hitting on her? What if Ronnie decided he would be better to hang out with than me? She didn't know him. I didn't know him either, but I had his number. Arje Dekker was one mean bastard.

I looked again and saw that they were gone. Shit. I walked over to where they had been talking, toeing the flattened grass where they had stood. I cursed Veronica for making me angry and for running off with a dangerous man she knew nothing about. Then I cursed myself for acting like a ten-year-old.

"There you are!" a male voice said behind me. I

turned to find Vic and Ronnie standing there like old chums.

"You were looking for a rematch?" I asked casually.

"The two of you know each other?" Veronica asked.

Dekker nodded. "He tossed me to the ground like a rag doll earlier." He stuck out his hand. "Arje Dekker."

I shook it. It would look too strange if I didn't. "Cy Bombay."

"Ronnie tells me you are here for the same reason I am."

Ronnie? He calls her Ronnie already? That's my nickname for her!

"I figured that out when I helped you up earlier." I forced a grin.

Something dark flashed in Arje's eyes. I recognized it. I'd seen it many times before. People who didn't have a conscience tended to look that way. I was grateful to see it. It reminded me who he really was.

"I thought it might be good to interview you together." Veronica held up her notebook as if that explained everything. "You might have some similar experiences."

"Maybe later . . ." I mumbled.

"After your next fight then. Before we leave with the others," she said firmly. At least I was happy to hear that she was still planning on staying with me.

"We'll see." I broke off and walked back to the others. I did not want to be around Dekker any more than I had to. The whole idea of being interviewed with that man was more than I could handle.

I thought of the look in Veronica's eyes . . . like she'd just hit the jackpot. That was troubling. The fact that Dekker was in the country and would be around wasn't the problem. The problem was Ronnie. She knew him now. When he died, she might even feel sorry for him. This was a complication I was not used to. Instead of just killing him, I'd have to find a way to make it look like something else. I'd done it before, but it was outside my comfort zone.

After rejoining Yalta and Zolbin, I decided to use my anger in the upcoming fight. The idea burned inside me like a white-hot brand. My energy started to rise and I pictured defeating Dekker over and over, using every trick Yalta had taught me. I knew I wouldn't face him again—he'd lost his one chance. But pretending it would be that slime bag seemed to help. I could actually feel my aggression spiking.

My first chance at this contest was a lucky one. The next opponent would be much tougher, and I had to get it together. Forcing everything else from my thoughts, I concentrated on my upcoming match and allowed the bloodlust to take over my senses. I felt sorry for the poor guy who would get me. He might win, but he'd be missing body parts. And that felt a little satisfying.

Chapter Thirteen

Rusty: How was the clink? You get the cookies I
  sent?
Danny: Why do you think I came to see you first?
—*Ocean's Eleven*

"Whatcha doing?" asked a distinctly familiar voice into my right ear as I watched the following matches from the sidelines. I didn't jump with surprise. Bombays don't do that. But I was a little more than surprised to see my cousin Missi standing next to me.

"Hey, cuz," I said. "What brings you to the farthest reaches of the planet? In the neighborhood and thought you'd say hi?"

She threw her arms around me with affection and I squeezed back. Truth be told, I wasn't all that startled. The family had a way of popping up where you least expected them.

"Business," she said. Missi was a bit older than me, with two teenage sons. She was cute with her short, messy hair and eyes that never missed a thing. She was the Bombay family's inventor of weapons—something that had saved my ass on more than one occasion.

"Business, eh? So are you the one who slipped me the envelope?"

She shook her head distractedly. "No. Monty and Jack did it." She craned her neck to the left. "You haven't seen them, have you?"

Wow. There were a whole mess of white people in this little hamlet. That would be hard to explain to the locals.

"No."

"What's up with the panties?" she asked, turning her attention back to me.

"Uniform. They are supposed to make movement less restricted."

"I see." And actually, I think she did.

"Why are you here, Missi?" The question did beg to be answered.

She smiled at me and I laughed. Missi had this kooky sort of presence that made her incredibly lovable . . . like a deranged Muppet. Underestimating her, however, could be deadly. She once created a bicycle helmet fitted with a pneumatic bolt gun that pierced the brain of its victim, killing him on the first leg of the Tour de France. She managed to switch out helmets while acting like a concerned Good Samaritan. They never did figure that one out.

"Mom wanted you to have this." Missi handed me a cell phone.

"I have a cell phone."

She shook her head. "Not like this one. I guess you probably noticed that your cell doesn't work here."

I nodded. And it hadn't bothered me.

"This phone uses Russian and Chinese satellites."

Missi popped open the phone to show me an expanding screen inside, complete with QWERTY keyboard. "You can communicate with us in real time via video. That way the council can keep track of you." She winked, indicating that she knew I wouldn't like that.

"I'm not happy about this job," I said. "Vic is too close. He's getting to know my friends here. I don't like that. And the last thing I need is the council breathing down my neck."

Missi nodded. "Seems we've been getting more of these types of assignments lately. I blame the Internet. There's no anonymity anymore. Just one huge global community center."

"That doesn't help me." I scanned the crowd and noticed several people looking our way. "People are starting to notice you. You'd better head out."

Missi glanced around. "Well, we're off. I promised the kids we'd hit Tokyo on the way home for some tech stuff." She walked a few steps away, then turned back. "Oh, and could you get me some good cashmere yarn? Or maybe a felted bag? Thanks!" And with that, she was gone.

Most people might be a little unsettled by such a visit. But most people weren't Bombays. The question was, how had she found me? There was a rumor that ran through our generation that Missi had somehow implanted us all with either tracking or explosive material. After this little family visit, I was beginning to believe in the former.

I looked at the phone in my hand. My next fight would start in a few minutes and I was wearing nothing but panties, boots and sleeves. Where in the hell was I going to put it?

"Cy!" Sansar-Huu called, indicating that it was my turn to wrestle. Great. I shoved the phone in my boots, hoping it was sturdy enough to survive the fight. Kicking wasn't really part of the game.

I had to push my conversation with Missi (and wondering how she and the boys got in and out of there unnoticed) out of my thoughts or I wouldn't win this fight. As I did the eagle dance and slapped my thighs, I'd rekindled my anger toward Dekker. My opponent, a rather large man with maybe fifty pounds on me, grabbed my shoulders.

He didn't stand a chance as I threw him onto his knee, winning the match. Good thing I wasn't really angry or he might not have survived. As I stalked off mid cheers from my friends, my anger dissipated a bit.

"Who was that?" Ronnie asked as I slipped my *deel* back on. I'd have another match soon, but it was starting to get chilly and I was covered in sweat.

"The loser," I said shortly.

"No, the blonde." She looked upset. It took me a second to realize what she was talking about.

"Oh, that." What was I supposed to tell her? That my cousin from South America dropped by for a quick visit and to drop off a cell phone you could bounce off Chinese satellites?

"Yeah, that." Veronica folded her arms and I almost laughed.

"Another grad student working on a thesis," I lied.

Her face contorted for a moment as she wrestled with this information. I can't say I didn't enjoy that.

"Who is she?" Ronnie tried again. I would've been surprised if she hadn't.

"Some woman." That was technically true. The fact that I knew her wasn't necessarily important.

"One of your 'groupies'?" I could swear I actually saw the words in frost hovering in the air.

"Yeah. I have blonde, wealthy, bored-housewife followers here."

"Are you sleeping with her?"

Wow. This chick didn't give up. I couldn't remember ever having someone jealous or possessive over me.

"I can honestly say I've never had sex with that woman." True.

"I—" she began.

"Veronica." My tone turned to ice. "I've had enough. Drop it." I stalked past her before I would have to throw her to the ground. Besides, she'd now empowered me with enough anger to win the whole damned competition. I wanted to keep it that way.

"Keep her," I said to Chudruk, "away from me." I pointed at Ronnie. My wingman nodded solemnly. Women could be a huge distraction in sports. I didn't wait to see how he would do this as I headed for Zerleg and Zolbin. My new cell phone rubbed uncomfortably against my shin. I'd had enough of women for the day.

My next two matches lasted mere seconds as I bartered my fury for victory. It was my third fight that didn't work out. I tripped over my own feet and fell to the ground. Exhaustion, mental and physical, was getting the best of me. I shrugged on my *deel* and climbed into the truck and passed out without talking to anyone.

A jolt brought me bolt upright and I found that the truck was moving.

"You're awake." Sansar-Huu laughed.

I looked around. The two of us were the only ones in the cab. Dark shapes murmured quietly from the back.

"Where's Ronnie?" I panicked a little, worried that she might have opted out of coming back with us. But where would she go? My nerves tightened as I thought she might have gone off with Dekker. That man was a killer.

"In the back," Sansar-Huu said. "She was mad at you and decided to sit there."

I leaned against the headrest in relief. I'd been hard on her. If she went with my vic, all kinds of terrible things might have happened. Even worse, she might have slept with him.

That stopped me. Why did I care about that? I'd just spent the trip down here informing Ms. Gale that I was no virgin. I didn't really think she was. But the thought of someone else having her was like a cheese grater running over my stomach.

I didn't say much the whole trip. It was probably my mood that kept the driver quiet too.

I was in my *ger*, stripping off my *deel* as Veronica walked in and threw her notepad on her cot.

Turning toward her as I took off my sleeves and boots, I asked, "Well?"

Ronnie looked me up and down and actually gulped. I was wearing only the "panties," as Missi called them. I was in great shape and I knew it.

She crossed her arms over her chest. It was kind of a turn-on. "I suppose you are expecting an apology?" she said. Her tone indicated that I wasn't going to get one.

I hooked my thumbs in the front of my pants. Veronica gasped, as if worried I was going to rip them off right there. I toyed with that very idea before crossing the room, taking her into my arms and kissing her.

She resisted at first, but I held firm. Her body hardened against mine and all rational thought was overridden by desire. Apparently, the same thing overwhelmed her also, because she kissed me with everything she had. In fact, I was a bit shocked to find a tiger in my arms.

Veronica Gale ran her hands through my hair, twisting her fingers through it. I reacted the only way I could: Reason fled and my hands slid down her back and waist to her taut, round ass. I pulled her hard against me. She acknowledged my arousal with a moan that melted my spine and set fire to my brain.

Sliding my fingers upward I pulled her sweater up and over her head with a firm yank. The need burning in her eyes caught me off guard and drove me completely mad. I unfastened her bra and pulled it from between us. She gasped again, a sound that was quickly becoming the most erotic I'd ever heard. Her full, perfect breasts throbbed, and she took a ragged breath. I gently palmed each nipple. I wanted her more than I'd ever wanted anyone.

Ronnie spun me around, pushed me to a sitting position on the cot and climbed on top of me. I took her right breast into my mouth as she ground her pelvis against mine, driving me crazy. Running my tongue over her nipple, I felt a tidal wave of emotion well up inside me. This was going to be way more than just some casual sex.

"Ohhhhh . . ." Ronnie moaned, and the tidal wave turned into a monsoon.

With one movement I had her beneath me. I don't even remember our clothes coming off, just this sudden sensation that I was inside her. As I looked down into her eyes, I saw for the first time a completely carefree Veronica.

This made me ache for her. I wanted more, even though that was physically impossible at the moment. Taking my time as I moved, I studied her features. She was warm and open, possibly for the first time with me. It was as if Veronica gave up fighting me for once. It was a heady feeling no wine could ever produce.

She cried out as she came, and the sensation quickly brought me to my climax. Veronica glowed as she pulled me toward her for a kiss.

"I think we should fight more often," I said, snuggling her warm body against mine.

"That was pretty hot," she said.

I felt a sense of heavy satisfaction I couldn't remember experiencing before. This felt so right. Like all the stars were in perfect alignment. Like all was at peace in the universe. Sleep smothered me with its lumbering breath as I fell head over heels into something I could never, ever understand.

Chapter Fourteen

Agent 47: Because that suitcase holds perfectly my blazer sniper rifle, two .45s and a gag for talkative, irritating little girls like yourself. Do you want me to stop and get it out?

Nika Boronina: I don't know—Do you think we have time for foreplay?

—*Hitman*

The sound of the door of the stove creaking woke me up, and the first thing I noticed was that I was in the wrong bed and naked. The second thing I noticed was that I was alone. As I shifted under the covers, the scent of Ronnie's body gave me a drunken sensation of pleasure.

Ronnie was bent over the stove, feeding the fire. She wore nothing but her underwear, and as a result, I became hard as a brick. Raising myself up on my elbow, I watched her in silence before she noticed me and ran back into my arms.

Her skin was chilled and I did my best to warm her up. The panties came off with a flick of my wrist, and within moments I found myself deep inside of this woman. Words could not express the sensations I felt as I moved slowly within her. Ronnie's throaty moans only drove me harder and faster, and it seemed that we both came too quickly. Damn.

"Think we can play hooky today?" she murmured.

I laughed at her choice of words. Was everything related to school with her?

"I suppose I earned my stripes yesterday . . ." I answered.

She giggled and the sound went straight to my cock. "You earned more than that last night."

My arms circled her body. I wanted nothing more than to just hold her beneath the warm wool blankets in a tent in the middle of nowhere. It seemed so perfect.

"Is that your phone?" Veronica turned her face up to mine, and I realized that a phone was in fact ringing. She reached into my boot and pulled out the cell Missi had given me yesterday. It was playing "We Are Family" by Sister Sledge. Cute.

"How in the hell do you have a phone that works here?" Ronnie sat up as I pulled the cell from her grip. For a second I was distracted by the sight of the blankets falling off of her breasts. Sigh. They were certainly magnificent.

"Yes?" It took all my willpower to focus on the phone.

"Squidgy!" Mom squealed on the other end.

Veronica mouthed the word *Squidgy* with a sort of glee that told me I was a dead man later. I got out of the bed and walked to the other side of the *ger*.

"Hello, Mum." I thought I heard Ronnie giggling behind me but chose to ignore it. "What's up?"

"I just wanted to get a report and make sure you were warm enough out there." This, I knew, was code for the job. But anyone overhearing would just think my mother was concerned.

I looked back at the lusciously topless Veronica as she held herself to keep from laughing out loud.

"Don't worry, Mum. I'm keeping warm enough." This proved to be more than Ronnie could bear, and she burst out in howls.

"Squidge," Mum said slowly, "are you with a woman?" Good old Mum. She knew how I operated and yet avoided calling me a man-slut.

"Yes." I don't know why I bothered with the truth. It was certainly more than I'd ever given her before when she'd interrupted me with a woman.

Her voice changed. "You are with someone?" She said *someone* as if she were really saying *my future daughter-in-law and mother of my many, many grandchildren*.

"Yes." No point in giving the woman too much information or she might start ordering her mother-of-the-groom dress.

"So does that mean—" she started.

"It means I can't really talk right now," I cut in.

I could hear Dad yell, "Go get her, m'boy!" in the background. Lovely.

Mom hung up without saying good-bye. It was probably for the best, considering she'd be texting me soon for the correct spelling of Ronnie's name for the wedding invitations.

Bombays are a strange lot. As suspicious as we are about outsiders, nothing seems to thrill our killer mothers more than the idea of their children marrying and settling down to make more assassins. Maybe it's a business thing.

"How is Mum?" Ronnie asked with a grin.

"Mum who?" I said as I slid back into bed. The last person I wanted to think of as I dived beneath the covers for Ms. Gale's lovely pussy was my mother. Fortunately, I had no problem forgetting she ever existed.

"Cy?" Chudruk called from outside the tent a few hours later. I was too exhausted to answer. Ronnie turned out to be tireless in the sack. Much as I didn't want to leave that cot—ever—I figured I needed to replenish some vital bodily fluids or I would die.

"Are you dead?" My friend read my thoughts through the thick felt.

"Just a minute," I called as I carefully slid out from underneath a sleeping Veronica. I guess she had to recharge somehow. After putting on a T-shirt, shorts and tennis shoes I quietly joined Chudruk outside.

"You look like hell." He smiled. "Rough night?"

"And morning," I answered, running my hands through my hair. "Sorry I missed training." I looked back at the door. "I was detained."

Chudruk nodded. "It's okay. Everyone's taking the day off. I was coming to offer you the comfort of my goats, but I see you found other entertainment."

I laughed. "Yeah. I don't think I'll need goats for a while."

"Well, the offer still stands." He held out a cloth-wrapped bundle. My stomach growled in appreciation as I opened it to find bread, cheese and milk. I nodded and took the bundle inside to give my sleeping woman breakfast in bed.

Ronnie pushed her hair away from sleepy eyes. "Was that Chudruk?" She smiled when she saw the food.

"Yes," I answered as I handed her the cup of milk. "He had a tempting offer, but I told him I was giving up goats for you."

"Wow. It's good to know I can hold my own against a couple of smelly goats," she said between sips.

I scratched my chin. "Oh, I don't know. These are cashmere-producing goats. Very rare and very expensive."

"Come on!" Ronnie rolled her eyes. "They're just goats."

Shaking my head, I replied, "Not really. You see, cashmere only comes from Mongolian and Chinese goats." I stroked her stomach. "The hair on their bellies creates pure cashmere. These goats can't live anywhere else in the world. And over the course of a year it takes three to four goats just to produce enough for one sweater."

Veronica looked at me strangely. "How do you know that?"

I swallowed my food before responding. "Knitter,

117

remember? And I love working with cashmere. It's really expensive, though."

She said nothing for a moment. "You know, every time I think I've got you pigeonholed, you completely freak me out."

"I'm not sure that's a good thing." If I had hackles, they would have been rising about then.

"When I say 'freaking out,' I don't mean to insult you," she started.

"I don't like the idea of being pigeonholed. Now, that's insulting." I kissed her on the forehead.

"Why would that insult you?" Veronica frowned as she got out of bed and started dressing.

"Because nobody should be a textbook anything. People are complicated. There's no black and white." I reached for Sartre, who began *wheek*ing loudly, presumably for breakfast. "The fact that you thought you had me pegged when you first met me shows how wrong you turned out to be."

"Wrong?" There was an edge in her voice that was hard to miss. "There are entire behavioral sciences built around categorizing people. Just because you are so different doesn't mean the majority of people are."

"Different? You mean because I'm an overeducated carney who likes to knit and study different fighting styles? You know more about me than almost anyone else, and you still don't know me as well as you think you do."

She was getting mad now. It was obvious in the way the large carotid artery throbbed in her neck.

"Oh, I don't know you, do I? Even you are predictable in some ways."

Oh, really? Would she even guess that I'm an assassin?

I watched her as she pulled out some notebooks and opened them on her cot. Apparently she was ending this conversation with the last word and planning to engross herself in her work to shut me out.

"People aren't predictable. We just like to think that because it makes us feel safer." I walked over to her cot and picked up a folder. "Take this guy—Senator Anderson. I mean, what do we really know about him?"

Ronnie snatched the file out of my hands. "Senator Anderson was a great man! He was going to change the world!"

Wow. She went from zero to white-hot in seconds. Apparently I'd touched a nerve.

"His life was an open book!" she sputtered. "Unlike you!" Veronica slammed her notebook shut just before she stalked out of the *ger*. I picked up her file on Anderson, then looked back at the door.

Within just a few hours, I'd managed to seduce this girl and piss her off to volcanic proportions. I really did have a way with women.

Chapter Fifteen

Debi: I should have worn a skirt.
Marty: I should have brought a gun.
—*GROSSE POINTE BLANK*

Ronnie's folder was a loving homage to a dead politi-
cian. I remembered when I first heard of Senator Anderson. He'd been campaigning at a county fair I was
working about ten years ago. William Anderson was a
small-town nice guy who spoke from the heart in
plain English fused with common sense. Many people
compared him to Kennedy with his youth, good looks
and optimism. Others saw him as a down-home Bill
Clinton. Whatever side you agreed with, almost everyone thought he was presidential material right
from the start.

I remember seeing him talk while I ran the Tilt-
A-Whirl. The man definitely knew how to work a
crowd. And people liked him. He crusaded against
big business and corporate America. Anderson came
from blue-collar roots and it showed. And everywhere
you looked, he was followed by a throng of college students eager to be part of his mission.

I couldn't blame them. I liked him too. I just wasn't
into politics. Not my thing. Oh, I can chew on an

idea for weeks. But politics frustrate me. Not because I can't understand them . . . but rather because I do. And then there was the fact that politicians occasionally showed up on the Bombay hit lists. That was part of the problem.

It didn't surprise me that Veronica had been a follower of Anderson's. There was a lot to like about the man. I'd like to think that if he'd lived, he might have made the changes he spoke of. But the fact of the matter was, he didn't. Senator William Anderson had died of a heart attack before he'd had a chance to take the national stage. And the country mourned him as his most ardent supporters cried out conspiracy theories.

"I never said he wasn't a good man," I murmured. Veronica tried to slip into the *ger* unnoticed, watching me as I read her folder.

"You questioned his ideas," she said as she took long strides to where I stood and snapped the folder from my grasp.

I looked her right in the eyes. "So?"

"What do you mean by that?"

"He's just a man. That's all." It irritated me that she had this dead guy on a pedestal. Life was for the living.

"He could've changed the world. And he was cut down in his prime."

I sat on her cot. "So, you are one of the conspiracy theorists, eh?"

Ronnie turned sharply toward me. "It's not a theory. There's a lot of evidence that says he was murdered."

That was something I did understand, in a way. After all, the Bombays have been pretty good about hiding their tracks over the centuries and have tended to be at the center of some conspiracies. It's the nature of the game.

"Ah, but which conspiracy? The right? The left? Fundamentalists? There are so many."

Ronnie sat next to me. "Don't make fun of me, Cy. This is something I've always felt very strongly about."

"I can see that."

"If they can kill a man like that, what hope is there for someone else to come along and take his place?"

"That's a pretty bleak thought."

"I believed in him. I volunteered with the campaign. When I wasn't studying, I was campaigning. It was my whole life."

"That's not much of a life. Living only for other people."

She didn't say anything. I felt bad about arguing with her. It was pretty obvious I had cut her to the quick.

"I'm sorry. I have a talent for being argumentative." It comes with a philosophy degree. Or maybe people who argue just tend toward philosophy. And sometimes they become lawyers. Unfortunately, there's nothing I can do about that.

Veronica stared at me and, deciding I was worthy of continuing the conversation, began, "My parents died in an explosion. I wasn't really raised by family so much as shipped off to school. I loved learning, but people came and went in and out of my life too much. When Senator Anderson came to town, I found a family in his other supporters. And I really believed in him."

I took her hand, stroking her fingers as they rested in my palm. "He had a heart attack. It happens."

She waved her hand over the papers on her cot. "I've been researching his death for years. I'm convinced he was murdered. And someday I will prove it."

"And you are doing this in addition to your thesis? That's a lot to take on."

She nodded. "Well, as you've seen, I don't have much of a social life. Mongolia is the first time I've been outside the United States."

"I hope you've learned something here." And I did, too.

"Yes and no." Ronnie didn't add to that, and I decided not to push her.

"I'll help you." Now, why did I say that? That was strange.

Her eyes flicked up to mine. "What do you mean?"

"I mean that I'll help you. I'll help you with your thesis, and I'll help you with your investigation."

She stood up quickly. "Why? Why would you do that?"

I stood also. "I don't know. Maybe because I've been a dick. Maybe because I have feelings for you. Maybe I've been knocked on my ass too much lately. The fact is, I said I'd help you and I will."

Veronica threw her arms around me. "Thanks, Cy."

As I buried my face in her hair, I wondered what the hell I'd gotten myself into.

"The *naadam* is just a few days away," Chudruk was telling me as I nursed a bruised shoulder. Zerleg, Zolbin and I were now training together, and those boys were a lot younger than I was.

"I know. Look, I didn't plan to win. I just wanted the experience," I managed through gritted teeth. My shoulder might have been sprained. And that would suck.

He shook his head. "That is obvious." He ducked as I playfully tossed my hat at him. "Yalta wants you to stop messing around with Veronica."

He had my attention now. "What?"

A wide grin spread across his face. "It will sap your strength." He punctuated his less-than-great news with a shrug.

"Oh. I see." And I did. It was a typical requirement made of fighters in all types of disciplines, from boxing to martial arts. The idea was that sex before a fight took away your aggression, making you weak.

"No problem," I said, rising to my feet. "Tell my *zazul* not to worry."

Chudruk laughed as he walked away. He laughed even harder as he passed a very red-faced Ronnie as she came toward me.

"You'll never guess what Odgerel just told me!"

"That we had to cool it on the sex until after the

naadam?" I answered casually, as if I was asking for the time.

You know, I didn't think it was possible for a person to turn purple with embarrassment. Huh. I guess you really do learn something new every day.

"How . . . how . . ." the poor thing attempted.

"Because I just had the same conversation with Chudruk."

Veronica turned to look at the retreating man. "So that's why he laughed." She turned back to me. "Cy, this is humiliating! You mean to tell me they all know?"

Now it was my turn to laugh. "Really, Ronnie. We're not in high school. This is hardly scandalous information here."

"What does that mean?"

"It means we are adults. And in most cultures around the world, sex is a natural and casual thing." I felt a spike of pain in my shoulder and started to rub it.

Veronica walked around me and rubbed my shoulder for me. "Are you saying I'm a prude?"

"Yes." Uh-oh. The massage stopped. "And no." It started up again. "You certainly have no problem getting in the mood. But I think your experience with the way other cultures see sex is somewhat limited."

She said nothing, so I continued. "Remember your reaction to hearing about my sexual past?"

"Yes. I was shocked by the fact that you were some sort of gigolo."

That made me laugh. "A gigolo? I never accepted money. I think of it more as a rock star with groupies."

I couldn't see her, but I knew she was rolling her eyes behind me.

"Oh, yeah. A carney is just the same thing as a rock star." Was it possible to actually see sarcasm as it floated past you in the air?

"Well, something like that. Anyway, you just have to get past those Midwestern morals and loosen up."

She slapped me on the shoulder. It took everything I had not to wince. "I admit I'm a bit conservative about sex. And I admit that the romance of this place had its way with my mind . . . and body." She walked around to face me. "But I will certainly have no problem with celibacy over the next few days." Ronnie stuck her tongue out at me and walked away, swaying her hips as she went.

Somehow, I had the feeling that the gauntlet had been thrown. And I was going to lose.

Chapter Sixteen

Tony Stark: They say that the best weapon is the one you never have to fire. I respectfully disagree. I prefer the weapon you only have to fire once. That's how Dad did it, that's how America does it . . . and it's worked out pretty well so far.

—*IRON MAN*

Zolbin, Zerleg and I wrestled the rest of the afternoon. My shoulder burned with pain, but I blocked it out mentally. After a few hours I was favoring my good shoulder, and the boys were exploiting my injury to their advantage. Not that I could blame them. As Yalta had explained, any opponent would do the same thing.

After soaking in the ice-cold stream for a while, I wet a T-shirt and wrapped it around my joint. All the way back to my *ger*, I thought of nothing but the extra-strength aspirin I had smuggled in for something just like this. In combination with some hot tea and rest, I should be better in the morning.

I stepped into my tent and shut the door. Ronnie was playing with Sartre on a blanket on the floor. My mind was absorbed with finding the painkillers, and once I swallowed them, I sank down on my cot and unwrapped the rag from my shoulder. It was swollen and sore. But the meds would take care of that. I turned my attention to my tentmate and stopped cold.

Ronnie smiled seductively. How I'd failed to notice she was naked was beyond comprehension. The woman was actually nude on a blanket in front of me. I started toward her.

She held up her hand to stop me. "No sex, remember?"

I started to peel off my shorts. "Oh, I'm not worried about that superstition."

"But I am. And *no* means *no*."

"Then why are you laid out like a flesh buffet?" I loosened the stays on the *shuudag*.

"Me?" Her eyes grew wide in feigned innocence. "I was just overly warm." Her hardened nipples and goose bumps said otherwise. I sat down on the floor next to her.

"Now who is thinking like a puritan? Nudity is not as important in other cultures, Cy."

I was one breath away from her. The scent from her skin made not touching her unbearable. I pulled her onto my lap, her breasts pressing against my chest. If she was still serious about celibacy after feeling my cock against her, then I would—

"No." Veronica pushed off me and giggled as she scooped up Sartre and moved to her cot.

I sat there in complete confusion, not to mention sexual frustration. Was she for real? Apparently, the game was afoot. Ronnie was taking her vow of celibacy until the match was over to new heights by throwing in torture . . . just for fun.

You know those commercials for erectile dysfunction where they warn you about calling a doctor immediately if you have an erection that lasts more than four hours? Well, mine lasted for a lot longer than that. And the nearest doctor was too far away to visit. I was beginning to wonder if Ronnie had switched my aspirin with Viagra. At one point that night I was pretty sure I was hallucinating. Either that or there really was a telephone pole attached to my groin with seven bluebirds and a turkey buzzard sitting on it.

I would like to say that I could have justified her playful behavior. But every time I saw that sweet little ass or her bare shoulders (hell, even a naked elbow was driving me mad), I began to think I knew absolutely nothing about women.

In addition to my constant state of arousal, almost the entire camp was readying for the move to the outskirts of Ulaanbaatar for the national *naadam*. From rounding up the animals to taking down the *ger*s, everything was a flurry of activity. Even Veronica was too busy helping Odgerel to spend much time naked in our *ger*—a fact that made me eternally grateful. Yalta had stopped training to allow us to help.

Ronnie and I were to take down our own *ger*. And to my surprise, she was very excited about it. The hardest part for us was removing the felt cover. But once we had it off, collapsing the lattice frame and packing everything was fairly easy. We worked very well together. And that surprised me too.

Most of the women who'd wandered through my life over the past decade were mere sexual nomads at best. They joined me in my bed, then left. I was used to that. But none of them ever hung out with me, did chores with me, or even engaged in everyday conversations with me. Sure, there were one or two women on the carney circuit. But I never really worked with them directly, nor did I get involved with them physically. I wondered why that was now, but I never did at the time.

There was something so simple, yet amazing about spending time this way with Veronica Gale. On this trip, we could be working on chores side by side one moment, then committing all sorts of carnal delights in bed the next. And we were together all the time. There was nowhere to go on a proper date. No movie theaters, no fine dining, no computers, television or radio even. Just two people in the wilderness.

I didn't know what would mess with my brain more: the relationship or the purity of the whole thing.

"And we should have dinner with Arje when we get to the city." Veronica interrupted my thoughts on Veronica as we hauled the stove to the truck.

"What?"

"You know, Arje Dekker? We met him at the last *naadam*. I think he was Danish or something."

"Dutch," I said absently. Now, there was another problem entirely. I still had my assignment to take out Dekker. My complications had just taken on complications for themselves. "I don't know if we will have time," I mumbled.

"Of course we will. We'll be there for three days!" She was careful to punch me playfully in my good shoulder.

"We might not even run into him." I had to discourage her from the idea of hanging out with my vic. At some point, Dekker would be dead and Ronnie would probably be somewhat pissed off about that.

She stopped and put her hands on her hips. "Cy! You said you would help me with my thesis. And Dekker will add another dimension to it."

"I know, but . . ." Damn. I had said that.

"You promised." Ronnie narrowed her eyes and it sort of turned me on. Hell, everything she did turned me on lately. She was in for one hell of a six-hour-long ride when this whole thing was over. I might even throw my first match just to spend the rest of the festival naked in her arms—I was that desperate.

"Fine. If we see him, we can make some plans for lunch or something. But that's it."

I was grateful when she accepted this with a smile and we continued working. However, I had the sneaking suspicion it was far from over.

Chapter Seventeen

"It doesn't say . . . yeah, we killed him. But trust us,
this guy was horrid."

—GERMAN SS OFFICERS SKIT,
MITCHELL & WEBB

The only good thing about the conversation about
Arje Dekker was that now I had to plan his death—
and that worked like saltpeter on my exploding libido.
As I helped load everything onto camels, horses and
one pickup truck, I worked on how I would dispatch
this asshole. There were a lot of problems with this
particular hit.

First of all, I was competing. My focus should be
on the match, not the job. Second, Veronica was
friendly with Dekker. Because of this, the hit would
have to be after the interview but before the end of the
festival, so he didn't get away. And I'd have to make
sure she didn't know about it. Third, my usual modus operandi wasn't going to work here. It would have
to look like an accident. For Ronnie's sake. The last
thing I needed was to provide her with another conspiracy to stalk. She would find out about Dekker's
death sometime, because of the Internet and her abil-

ity to do research. It was a given that she would look him up.

I toyed with the idea of "accidentally" snapping his neck in competition. It would be tough. As I'd learned already, each micromovement was critical. Dekker would have to fight in a way that would allow me to overpower him. And that was a total gamble. It went without saying that I would have to somehow manipulate the assignments to be matched up with him . . . a near impossibility here, where nothing was computerized.

If the opportunity presented itself, I could attempt it. But I had to have other options with better odds. Maybe I could maneuver the lunch date to happen at the conclusion of the festival. If I played my cards right, I could find out where he was staying and when he was leaving. Then, after escorting Ronnie back to our friends, I could slip back and kill him.

That seemed more reasonable. But how exactly would I do it to make it look like either an accident or natural causes? If I knew his weaknesses, whether physical or psychological, I could exploit them. Unfortunately, the file had no information where this was concerned.

An idea presented itself. I slipped away from the others and dug the cell phone Missi had given me out of my coat.

"Hey, Cy." Missi didn't sound like her usual, kooky self.

"You all right, cuz?"

She sighed. "I'm a contestant on an upcoming *Survivor*-type reality show. So, in answer to your question, not really."

"Why would you do that?"

"For work, of course."

Must be an assignment. But even though it sounded intriguing, I didn't have time to ask.

"Sorry to get to the point of the call, but can you forward me some medical info on my friend?" Chinese and Russian satellites be damned; this line was still far from secure. Fortunately, the Bombays learn how to say a lot with a little from an early age.

"I'll see what I can do and text it." Missi hung up. Back to business.

"Worried about the match?" Zerleg asked. I didn't even know he was there. Some catlike reflexes I have.

"No," I answered truthfully.

The teenager sat down on the grass beside me. I took this as a sign that he wanted to talk, so I joined him.

"What is it, kid?" I asked with a smile, trying to lighten the mood.

"Nothing," he answered. Which in teenage boy talk meant, *Everything*.

"Right."

"It's just . . ." Zerleg started. "It's just that I don't know why I am doing this."

I admired his grasp of English. There was an accent there, but his grammar was flawless.

I crossed my legs. Might as well be comfortable. "I assumed you were doing it because you wanted to."

"I did. And I do." He waved me off and rose to his feet. "I just have cold feet. Thanks for listening, though."

I watched as he walked back to the others, hands thrust deep inside his pants pockets. As much as I wanted to be a good friend to Zerleg, I was grateful he hadn't confided everything. I didn't need any more drama on this trip. For the first time since I'd arrived, I was actually looking forward to going home.

The next morning the entire camp began to move out. Sansar-Huu, because it was his truck, drove Yalta, Zerleg, Zolban and me to get us there early for some last-minute training. Veronica, to my surprise, insisted on traveling with Odgerel and the others. It was a gesture that made my heart skip a beat. I remembered when she arrived and was so worried about being lost in this foreign place. Now she was one of them. I liked that.

I sat in the back with the boys, insisting that Yalta have the passenger seat. Cool breezes dried our perspiration from the hot sun as we drove through the countryside to the city. Zolban was in high spirits—probably due to his success in the previous competitions. Zerleg was silent. Moody almost. Since we would be in the truck for a long time, I decided to ask him about the conversation we almost had.

"Oh, it was nothing," Zerleg said over the wind.

Zolban laughed. "No, it is not!"

Zerleg looked quickly from me to his brother and told him to shut up in Mongolian.

"Do you want to talk about it?" I asked casually, hoping my tone would seem inviting.

"Go ahead!" Zolban punched his brother in the arm. Zerleg looked away.

"He wants to go to university," his brother told me.

"That's good," I replied.

"Not good," Zolban said eagerly. Clearly he relished his role of tattletale. "His girlfriend doesn't like it."

"Oh. I see." Zerleg looked up at me sheepishly as I spoke.

He took over for his brother. "She wants to live on the steppes. She thinks my wanting an education is stupid."

"But you want to go to school, right? Be a poet?"

He nodded.

"Can't she come with you? Or visit during breaks?" I suggested.

"I don't want her to. I want to meet other people. See the world." Zerleg wasn't meeting my eyes now.

"You don't love her?" I asked gingerly.

The boy shook his head. "We do not have anything in common. I am not interested in her." He leaned forward. "What would you do?"

Both boys looked at me eagerly, as if I would dispense words of wisdom on this matter. I used to be confident about women. But ever since Veronica Gale

stormed her way into my life I was pretty sure I now
knew less than nothing.

"What do your parents think?" That sounded like
an intelligent way to stall. Technically, I was still an
outsider, and the family would probably frown on any
influence I had over the boys.

"Bah!" Zerleg spit. "They want me to stay here too.
Like Sasug, they want me to be a sheepherder."

"Sasug?" I asked, a little confused. "Doesn't that
mean 'smelly'?" Maybe my Mongolian wasn't that
good.

Zolban nodded. "Yes. But it actually means 'she
smells good.' At least, that is why they named her
that."

The boys seemed confused by my confusion, so I
let the matter drop. I'd never really gotten the hang of
Mongolian names and their various shades of meaning. All I could do was continue my profound respect
for their culture and leave it at that.

"Have you told your family how much this means
to you?"

Zerleg nodded. "Grandfather and Uncle Chudruk
are on my side. But they have little influence."

I had not met the boys' parents or Sasug. They
had not accompanied them on this journey. Zolbin
said they would be at the *naadam*, though, so I
wanted to be careful what advice I gave. Besides,
who would listen to advice from a single carney/as-
sassin whose most meaningful relationship had been
with a guinea pig?

"I think your grandfather is a wise man and can help you," I answered.

"What would you do?" Zerleg pressed. "If I were your son, what would you say?"

I thought about this a moment. "I would tell you to follow your heart," I said, hoping they would get it.

They didn't.

"What do you mean?" Zolbin asked. Apparently, he had a stake in this too.

"You should pursue what you love, and not what you don't. By marrying a woman you do not love and working at something you do not enjoy, you are hurting everyone. If you love education and poetry, you should pursue them both."

Zerleg's face brightened and he threw himself into my arms. And although I was glad he was happy, I wondered if this was going to bite me in the ass later. One more thing to add to our trip—a couple of angry parents and one pissed-off girlfriend. Not good.

Chapter Eighteen

Pamela Landy: This is Jason Bourne, the toughest target that you have ever tracked. He is really good at staying alive, and trying to kill him and failing . . . just pisses him off.

—*The Bourne Ultimatum*

The road to Ulaanbaatar was paved with trucks, yaks and horses. The sights and sounds were an exotic tonic for my nerves. I should say that I usually do not get nervous. However, I usually do not have this much going on. I tried to scan the crowds as we moved toward the edge of town, on the very slim chance that I could spot Dekker and maybe take him out before Ronnie arrived. No such luck.

Plan A was to ambush him. Missi still hadn't sent me any information, and I was on edge. There was always the old standby of slipping on a banana peel (which has worked so many times it's ridiculous) or falling in the bathtub, but I wasn't sure I could maneuver it after all the wrestling (or if he was staying someplace with an actual bathtub) . . . if I was lucky enough to advance through the competition.

In the end, I'd do whatever I could to finish the job. There was no other option. And if it had to look like foul play, I could make sure Ronnie knew how bad this guy was. Damn, this woman was making my usually mess-free life a mess.

As we pulled into the campground area, I found these worries slipping away. It was as if the world exploded in color. The brilliant blue sky fused with the blindingly green grass. People were covered in bright silks of every color imaginable. The cool air softly mingled with the heat from the sharp sun. Sounds of music and laughter competed with the smells of food and beer. It was home to me. A carnival. I felt like I belonged.

Yalta barely waited for the truck to come to a complete stop before he hurried us into a practice session. In fact, men were wrestling all around us as we went through our routine, warming up muscles that were tense from riding in a beat-up truck down bumpy roads for hours on end.

My shoulder was feeling better, and that gave me a small surge of confidence. I'd need it. All the wrestlers around us looked either a lot younger or a lot bigger than me. There was no doubt they all had more training too.

"Focus, Coney!" Sansar-Huu swiped me on the back of the head playfully, and I resumed my workout.

Something about hard work in the hot sun surrounded by bloodthirsty, happy people made me feel stronger. By the end of our training session I was spent but relaxed. Sansar-Huu shoved a cold glass of beer in my hands and I gulped it down. I'd really missed cold beer. That seemed to make the carnival setting complete.

"Hey! Cy!" Veronica's voice gave me a little shiver I was not prepared for. I turned to see her walking toward me. Her smile filled me with something I hadn't felt in decades.

"Look what Odgerel made for me!" She spun around in a silk *deel* the color of an orange sunset. The trim was brown fur, and for some reason this made her green eyes sparkle. I was stunned. Ronnie looked lovely in it. Ironic, isn't it? The *deel* covered everything. And yet she'd never looked more beautiful.

I pulled her hard against me, kissing her deeply. She responded to my body, and it occurred to me that I might need her *deel* to cover my arousal. But I couldn't let go of her lips, her body. I was pretty sure she wouldn't be able to say no tonight.

Veronica sighed and buried her face in my chest. I just held on to her, afraid to let her go . . . go where?

"Oh!" She laughed as she finally pushed away. "I forgot to tell you! Arje is here!"

Well, that was a buzz kill. And I wouldn't need her *deel* to cover me anymore. "Great," I managed.

"We're going to meet him for a drink! Come on!" With a smile that cut right through me, she dashed off into the crowd.

I barely managed to shrug on my *deel* before I spotted the two of them sitting on a blanket by the tent with the beer.

"Sit down!" Ronnie motioned me toward her.

"Dekker." I nodded my greeting and extended my hand. I had promised Veronica I would help her, and a simple courtesy was as much as I could do. Besides, the sooner she interviewed him, the sooner I could kill him.

"Bombay." Dekker took my hand and shook amiably enough, but there was a deadly caution in his eyes. I couldn't blame him. Why shouldn't he be suspicious of me? If he really knew what I was going to do to him in the next two days . . .

"I told him about my thesis, and Arje agreed to an interview," Ronnie was saying to me. I pulled myself out of my thoughts of murder and became the nice guy she knew me to be.

"So, Ronnie says you're a carney?" Dekker asked.

It pissed me off that he used my nickname for her. And it pissed me off that she didn't mind it.

"Yes. A carney with a strange obsession for fighting methods." I laughed forcibly. "So what is it you do?" Normally I don't ask Europeans that. They consider a question like that to be extremely rude. For once, I didn't mind playing the obnoxious American.

"Oh, I'm in the military . . ." he answered blithely.

Of course he wouldn't say he was a bloodthirsty mercenary who had taken the lives of women and children for the highest bidder. The intel I'd had on him mentioned an episode of ethnic cleansing he'd engineered in Africa that involved mutilated mothers and children who had been left to struggle for their next breath as he fled the country to his vacation home in the Bahamas with a suitcase full of euros.

"Really? That's amazing!" Veronica cried. "I could use a proper military perspective on my thesis."

I hated that she gushed over him without knowing the monster he truly was. It took everything I had to remain calm and casual on the outside.

"Damn," Ronnie said. "I wish I'd brought my digital recorder." Her face brightened. "I could run back and get it!"

I interrupted before she could leave me alone with this bastard. If she did, she'd just find him in pieces when she returned. And I couldn't have that.

"Let's just make plans to meet up again," I said quickly. "I'd like to get back to camp and rest for a bit." I turned to Dekker. "My *zazul*'s been working us since we got here. Don't know about you, man, but I'm too old for this shit."

Dekker grinned. "I'm right there with you on that, Cy." He looked at Ronnie, taking her hand in his. "Say tomorrow around noon?" Before I could crush his spine (something my grandmother taught me how to do using my elbow), he bent to kiss her hand and strode off.

"You aren't jealous, are you?" Veronica asked as we made our way to the camp.

"Of course not," I answered. But I was. The thought of Dekker speaking intimately to her, touching her, drove me crazy.

"I think you are," she teased, and took my hand in

hers. It was soft and warm. Just like her body that first morning after making love all night. The tension in my shoulders released a bit.

"My shoulder is just bothering me," I lied. "Zolbin threw me and I think I sprained it."

Veronica frowned, then looked at my right shoulder. "Oh. Well, I'll take a look at it when we get back."

I laughed. "And just what are you looking for? Have you ever seen a sprained shoulder before?"

"No." She winked. "But I'm sure Odgerel has something involving goat intestines and yak urine that I can put on it to make you feel better."

I tightened my grip on her fingers. "Oh, I think you can do something better than that."

"No. I promised Chudruk."

This caused me to jerk to attention. "Chud? Why did you promise him that?"

"Because he has some money riding on your performance here."

I looked at her sidelong. "I didn't think a girl like you approved of gambling."

"Well, let's just say I've loosened up a bit in the last few weeks."

"Maybe you could give me a demonstration of how loose you are willing to be?"

She pushed me away. "Not if I want to lose the money I've bet on you too." Veronica laughed and ran toward our group. All I could do was stare. That woman was full of surprises.

Chapter Nineteen

[*Dilios is putting a patch over his eye*]
Spartan King Leonidas: Dilios, I trust that "scratch" hasn't made you useless.
Dilios: Hardly, my lord, it's just an eye. The gods saw fit to grace me with a spare.

—*300*

Veronica Gale spent the rest of the day tormenting me with her orange-silk-wrapped body. Odgerel actually did have a paste made of yak urine and some other questionable matter for my shoulder. Ronnie didn't even wrinkle her nose as she smeared the gunk on my shoulder. To my amazement, it worked.

The two of us wandered through the festival atmosphere of the *naadam*. Tomorrow the matches would begin, complete with opening pageantry featuring the rich culture of Mongolia. As we made our way through the maze of musicians, dancers, food vendors and people, I realized that I wasn't feeling homesick. Not that I ever did. But I always had a sense of the fact that I was away from home. To me, home was my trailer. It didn't matter where it was; that was my home.

Strange as it seemed, whenever Ronnie held my hand, I was transported back to my sense of home.

Apparently, a flesh-and-blood woman was taking the place of my sweet, tricked-out RV.

I pondered that idea only briefly. Philosophers, as I've mentioned before, have a tendency to overthink things now and then.

The sun was setting and we needed to head back to the campsite. There would be a loud, raucous dinner followed by an all-night party that would not include Zerleg, Zolbin or me. In fact, Yalta insisted that the three of us share a *ger* during the festival to eliminate any distractions. I had the sneaking suspicion he included Ronnie as a distraction. To her credit, she graciously accepted Odgerel's invitation to stay with her family. There would be no sex tonight.

It was difficult to sleep with all the noise around us. Okay, it was difficult for me to sleep. The boys passed out immediately and snored like they were dying. I tossed and turned. It was weird to share my living arrangements. Even worse, Sartre was staying with Ronnie. Sansar-Huu's children were smitten with her. I didn't even have the comfort of my pig.

Well, I knew one thing that would help me sleep. And I was pretty sure Veronica would give in if I could just get to her. I slid on my sweatpants and a T-shirt and slipped out of the *ger*.

In spite of the party that was still going on, it was pitch dark outside. No electric lights here. But that would make it easier to sneak into Sansar-Huu's *ger*. Now, where was it?

I tripped over various things as I stumbled in the direction of the tent. Everyone must either have been asleep or have moved to another location. I hoped Ronnie had decided to get some sleep. Of course, if I had my way, there wouldn't be much of that going on.

I was making my way around the side of the tent when I heard something behind me. There was nothing there. That wasn't unusual. People were all over the place, and the ones still up were probably drunk. I turned my attention back to the door of the *ger*.

I heard something whisk through the air and then my vision was flooded with stars and pain. I shot my arm out behind me instinctively, and I managed to grab the weapon. But whoever had been on the other end let go and disappeared before I could identify him.

"Cy?" Veronica stood in the doorway wearing a T-shirt and shorts. She was vertical, then horizontal. No, wait, I was horizontal. At least, that was what I was thinking as everything went black.

The *naadam* field was packed. Following an exquisite version of the eagle dance, I turned to face my opponent and slapped my thighs. The giant guinea pig before me did the same and we approached each other to begin. It was hard to get a grip on his silky hair. And he looked so cute I didn't really want to fight him. But I was here to win.

"Cy!" Chudruk must have slapped me. As I looked up into his face, I realized I'd been dreaming.

"I'm okay." I started to sit up but a blinding pain forced me back down. There was blood on my hands. I had been hit.

Sansar-Huu held up a thick branch. "He hit you with this. We found you when Veronica screamed."

Veronica was sitting beside me, her face twisted with concern.

"Someone hit me?"

"I didn't see who it was." Veronica grabbed my hand.

Odgerel started examining the wound on the back of my head. I could feel the heat from the lantern she held.

"You won't need stitches, I think," she said slowly. "But you should not wrestle."

Yalta came into the *ger*, and everyone went quiet. He examined my wound and looked into my eyes. Then he spoke to Chudruk in Mongolian. I think he said my testicles should be fed to the marmots. Man, I really needed to work on my language skills.

"Pop says you do not need to wrestle. The decision is up to you, though," Chudruk said solemnly.

I looked at all of them. It was generous of my *zazul*. And he did have two more athletes competing. On the other hand, I came all this way just to do this. I had trained for a month for an event that happened only once a year. These people—my friends—gave their hospitality to me.

"You shouldn't compete," Ronnie said firmly. "You

have a concussion at the very least. You need to see a doctor."

Sansar-Huu nodded and Odgerel clucked sympathy. Sartre peeked out of Ronnie's hands and gave a firm, loud, "Wheek!"

I got up and shook my head gently. "When is my first match?"

Yalta spoke to his son.

"Pop can arrange for you to fight later in the day. He has a friend here in Ulaanbaatar who is a doctor. I will go find him." And with that, Chudruk left. I grinned. He knew me so well.

"No!" Veronica shouted. "He's concussed! He could have brain damage."

I shook my head, which, by the way, hurt considerably. "This is a grappling sport. There won't be any more injury to my head. I can't let everyone down."

To my astonishment, Chudruk reentered the *ger* with a tall man in a red *deel*, carrying a satchel. How did he do that so quickly? Maybe I was really messed up to the point that hours had actually passed instead of minutes?

We were all quiet while he examined me. Dr. Baatar asked me the usual questions to determine my level of confusion. He looked at my pupils and inquired about the pain. When he finished, he closed up his bag.

"You seem to be all right. But I worry about that headache," he said in perfect English. "Other than that, you have no symptoms of vomiting, confusion or memory loss. Your pupils are not dilated." The doctor tapped his head. "But if the headache gets worse, no wrestling."

I watched as Yalta slapped him on the back and Chudruk walked him out. Ronnie was staring holes into me. That was one thing about relationships I did not miss: having another's will imposed on me.

"My friend." Sansar-Huu sat down beside me. "Are you certain of this?"

"It is not necessary for you to fight," Chudruk added. I hadn't even noticed he'd come back.

"Guys, look. I'm fine. I'm going to participate," I insisted. To my left, I could feel Veronica's eyes go into laser-beam mode.

Yalta nodded and left, as did everyone but Veronica.

"You cannot wrestle," she said once everyone had cleared the tent.

I reached around and gingerly touched the back of my head. It was tender, but the bleeding had stopped. The dried blood would have to be rinsed out before I fought. I didn't want my opponent to know I'd been injured. Fortunately, the doctor had not wrapped my head.

"I said," Ronnie repeated, "you are *not* going to wrestle."

"I heard you."

She sighed. "I can't stop you, can I?"

I turned to her. "Look, has it even occurred to you to wonder who hit me and why?"

That stopped her short. "Is that even important at this point? Is that why you are doing this? To show whoever it was that he didn't stop you?" Veronica threw her hands up in the air. "This is about pride?"

"Actually, no. I'm not that shallow. This is about the fact that I worked very hard to do this. It's not even about winning. It is about following through."

Her hands came to rest on her hips. "So it is about pride."

"No. It isn't. And don't tell me what to do."

"So you're like a child who does it because the parent says not to do it."

I cocked my head to the side. "You think of yourself as my parent? That's kinky. Especially for you."

"Uh, no. I don't. I just think you are being unreasonable and immature." Her voice took on a dangerous timbre.

"Or maybe I'm being responsible." I rose to my feet. Daylight was sparking under the doorway, and I needed to get back to my cot to rest. It took all of my strength to stride nonchalantly to the door.

Unfortunately, Veronica followed. "You are just plain stubborn. What is it with men?"

Her questions came and went unanswered as I concentrated on walking casually to my tent. Whoever had hit me, for whatever reason, might be watching. And yes, my stubborn pride wanted them to think I was just fine.

I opened the door to the *ger* and slammed it behind me in Ronnie's face. It was rude, but I needed some peace and quiet. The boys were gone, probably too excited about the festivities.

Ronnie didn't take the hint and entered the tent.

"Don't shut me out, Cy, just because I tell you something you don't want to hear."

I lay down on my cot and closed my eyes.

"Don't lie down! Aren't you supposed to stay awake with a concussion?"

"Veronica," I said through gritted teeth, "my head hurts, so I doubt I will get any sleep. I just need some time to concentrate on my training. I don't mean to be rude, but will you please leave me alone?"

The hostility in the air crackled expectantly. I wondered if Ronnie was the violent type who would hurl something at me. Instead, I just heard footsteps, then the banging of the door behind her.

I should've been focusing on my techniques and working out how I was going to fight with my balance off. Okay, so I had lied to everyone about how badly I was hurt. And yes, I was a stubborn bastard. The vanity of men . . . I've considered it personally and academically throughout my life. Well, at least I'd just given Veronica Gale, Ph.D. candidate, more material for her thesis.

This was exactly why I wanted to remain single. A relationship with a woman meant having someone around to tell me I was too weak or old or sick to do something I wanted to do. I liked danger. And a woman would try to talk me out of it. It was exhausting to think about.

What was I thinking, anyway? Getting involved with Veronica like that? It interfered with the basic tenet of my philosophy—freedom. The only female I was beholden to was an eleven-inch-long rodent who was dependent upon me for her needs. Sartre never criticized me. Okay, maybe I could tell the difference between her general noises and her unmistakable sarcasm. But she never held me back. Never pigeonholed me. Never, ever told me what I could not do.

Here I was, a free thirty-eight-year-old man. Sure, I had my Bombay job. But that allowed me freedom too. Freedom from a desk job and other responsibilities. And it paid very, very well. For the most part, I could come and go whenever I wanted to. I traveled the world to follow my interests on the slightest whim.

What the hell was I thinking, getting involved with Ronnie? A naive professional student with no tolerance for violence or the things I found interesting? What was I going to do when this was over? Move her into my trailer? Take her with me from carnival to carnival? The woman had goals! She probably wanted some professorship somewhere quiet and safe! I'd tried that once. It didn't work for me.

So who was going to win here? No one. One of us would have to give up what we loved. It was against everything I believed in to do that. And I would hate myself if she compromised her dreams for me. Even though I was lying down, my head began to throb even more.

And what about my job as an assassin? There was no way in hell Veronica would ever be able to accept that. How could I tell her that I killed people for a living? I suspected that even though I only killed really bad people, she would still have a major problem with that. My very nature was in direct conflict with every cell in her sweet little body.

There was no hope for marriage. The council gave everyone in the Bombay family until the next family reunion to let their spouse know about their job. Even if I timed it just so and had five years (the time between reunions), I would never have the courage to tell her. And that would spell her death sentence. The Bombays were pretty black-and-white about spousal acceptance.

Damn. I really screwed up this time.

Chapter Twenty

Indiana Jones: It's not the years. It's the mileage.
—*RAIDERS OF THE LOST ARK*

"Cy?" I could hear Chudruk's voice from the doorway. How long had I been thinking about all of this?

"Come in." There were other things I needed to be concentrating on.

"Pop got you a match for the end of the day." Chud sat on Zerleg's cot. "Veronica is watching the opening ceremony with the others."

I sat up. "Thanks. I think I really pissed her off."

He laughed. "Women, eh?" Chudruk scratched his chin. "You know, I think this is the first time I've ever seen you with a woman for more than two hours."

I tossed my hat at him. He ducked. "When do the boys fight?" I didn't want to talk about Veronica.

"Zerleg fights in the first round. Zolbin later." He looked at me thoughtfully for a moment. "Did Zerleg talk to you?"

I nodded. "About the girl? Yes." I wasn't sure I wanted to get into this conversation. It was a family affair, and I was the outsider. But it did give me something else to talk about than my problems at the moment.

"He's a good kid," Chudruk replied. He seemed to be talking to himself more than me. "I want to see him go to school in the States. He's smart. He should go to school."

"Well, you know how I feel about education." If I gave too much of an opinion, I might insult the family's stance.

"He said you encouraged him. I'm happy about that."

"What does Yalta want?" I was going for noncommittal here.

"He thinks he should go. He thinks Sasug, the girlfriend, has the face of a camel."

I laughed in spite of myself. "I guess some problems are universal."

"Well, it will work out. My brother and his wife will come around." He stood up and smiled. "You should get some rest. I'll come back for you about an hour before your match."

Chudruk left and I lay there in the muffled quiet. Then I reached for my cell phone and made a call.

"I heard you did well!" I slapped Zerleg on the back a few hours later as I stood in the arena with him and his brother. My head still hurt, but I had been energized at hearing how the boy won two matches that afternoon. Zolbin and I would fight later.

"Thanks, Cy!" Zerleg's face was glowing with glee. I couldn't help noticing he kept looking over at a small group of girls in the crowd. One of the girls was dressed in Western clothing, wearing a miniskirt, a black T-shirt and large sunglasses. She was a lovely Mongolian girl, probably from the city.

"Who is that?" I asked him.

"Oh!" His face turned red. "That is Opia! She is a university student here."

"I see."

Veronica was in the stands with the others. Only athletes and their *zazuls* were allowed on the field. Zolbin was jumping up and down. He was up next. I spotted Chudruk waving from the bleachers. Ronnie ignored me. I was grateful for that.

Yalta nodded at Zolbin and the two of them walked toward the field. Zerleg dragged his attention away from the giggling Opia. We watched anxiously as Zolbin did his eagle dance around his grandfather, then slapped his thighs and approached his opponent.

To my shock, it was Arje Dekker he was to fight. Looking quickly into the stands, for reasons I had yet to comprehend, I saw Veronica give the son of a bitch a little wave. Dekker nodded at her and my gut twisted.

Zolbin attacked aggressively, his usual modus operandi. Dekker did the same, refusing to take a defensive stance. This could go bad for the kid. Dekker had a lot of experience in offensive measures.

While the boy was younger and stronger, Dekker had presence of mind. Again and again I watched as

Zolbin attacked, looking for cracks in Dekker's facade. Arje countered every movement. He struggled to hold on, but maintained his stance. Zolbin was trying to wear him down. The two locked arms several times, holding still for agonizing minutes on end. My head pounded. I desperately wanted to see Dekker beaten. Zolbin pulled back, then charged again, nearly knocking his opponent off of his feet. The crowd was silent. No one seemed to know where this was going.

The boy reached for Dekker's thigh, lifting his leg from the ground, and threw him. I watched with great satisfaction as the Dutchman fell to the dirt with a thud.

"You did it!" Zerleg bounced into his brother's arms and the two embraced.

I didn't take my eyes off the field. Dekker rose slowly to his feet and dusted off his knees. He slowly looked up into the stands and smiled and nodded. I traced his gaze to Veronica, who smiled back, concern playing across her face. Concern that had recently been on that face for me.

I watched as he made a signal, pointing off the field. Then, to my anger, she nodded, stood up and walked away. Perfect.

It was especially galling because Arje Dekker was the primary suspect in my attack. The last person I wanted Ronnie going off with was someone who had sneaked up behind me and hit me over the head, leaving me to bleed out, unconscious, in the dark.

Then again, Dekker had no reason to attack me. He barely knew me. He certainly had no idea I was going to kill him. The Bombays were pretty good about things like that. Maybe he wanted Ronnie for himself? It seemed hardly likely he'd resort to a cavemanlike approach to knock me out of the competition.

And what about the weapon? Men like Arje didn't travel unarmed. If he wanted me gone, he would've stabbed me. It would be more effective and easier to make it look like some drunk tried to roll me for a few *tögrög* or even American dollars. Why use a tree limb? No, that didn't seem very likely.

So maybe it was just a chance mugging. A Westerner would be a prime target in any country. Even though I'd been at a few local *naadams*, there were many people here who didn't know I had Mongolian connections and would see me as an easy mark. It was late and dark when I had slipped from my tent. There were more than five hundred contestants and thousands of visitors here. Too many suspects to make it easy for someone to pursue.

"It is time, Cy." Chudruk clapped me on my back, snapping me back to the present. I glanced at the stands. Veronica wasn't there. She would not see me wrestle. Fine. It was going to be over after this anyway. So why did I feel so bad?

Making my way to the field, I tried to focus on the match. My opponent faced me and we slapped our thighs to begin. My mind fought to keep focused on what would happen.

He was a very large man, and in his eyes I could see he was ready. I had been careful to wipe away the dried blood from my wound. It would have stood out too much against my blond hair. My sore shoulder was red, but maybe he wouldn't notice. If he grabbed too hard, I would wince and it would all be over.

Unfortunately, the first thing he did was grab both shoulders. Pain shot through the injured one into my arm. I stood as still as I could in an attempt to show no pain. My arms were beneath him, so I brought them together, up and through his hold to break it. Sweat poured down my face as I struggled with the agony of using that shoulder. As the hold broke, I reached for his knee and pulled it up as hard as I could. He fell. It was a miracle. I stared in disbelief as he sat on the ground. Instinctively I reached down to help him up. My opponent took my hand and yanked in an attempt to right himself. Unfortunately I had offered him the wrong hand and my shoulder screamed. He patted me on the back and I walked toward Yalta, my features placid, not betraying the twisting pain beneath.

"I cannot fight again today," I said to Chudruk in short, gasping breaths.

"Is it your head?" he asked, his face dark with concern.

"No." I laughed bitterly. "No, it's the damned shoulder."

"But you must fight again, Cy!" Zolbin cried out. "You have to win again to qualify for tomorrow!"

I understood that. But I also understood that I still had to kill Dekker. But now my shoulder was dislocated, and it would only get worse if I continued to wrestle. The *naadam*, for me, was over.

Chapter Twenty-one

Verbal: A man can convince anyone he's somebody else, but never himself.

—*THE USUAL SUSPECTS*

I watched from the edge of the arena as Zolbin won his second match. The thrill was bittersweet. I knew I shouldn't be pissed. I had done what I'd come here to do and succeeded. But it was over. It had to be.

Dr. Baatar managed to pop my joint back into place, and I managed not to scream during the process. It was a minor victory, if a hollow one. I didn't feel sorry for myself. How many men got to do something like this? And I'd managed to win with multiple injuries. In the past, I would've considered this a perfect experience.

So why didn't I consider it that now? The boys were advancing and I was happy for them. Zerleg was up in the stands, flirting with Opia. I could only guess that they were talking about poetry by the way she looked at him. Good for him. Zolbin was off with his friends. Yalta made him swear off the beer, but I knew his buddies would be celebrating for him tonight.

Back at the *ger*, the three of us sat on our cots dissecting the boys' matches as I helped them plot their moves for the next day. I promised to cheer for them, and Yalta convinced me to be on the field to help him coach. That made me feel good. It also made me realize that I was no longer twenty-one. Hell, I'd be forty soon.

Yalta had accepted the passage of time and moved gracefully from athlete into his role as coach. When would I do the same thing? Was Veronica right? How long was I going to travel around the world, fighting men younger and better trained than me?

Whoa. This idea shook me to my core. I was aging. Me. In fact, I was considered old in most of the countries I trained in. And while my experience had helped me win today, my body had given out on me. Granted, the concussion was not an age thing, but the shoulder was. I listened to the boys as they fell asleep, oblivious to all but victory and glory. They weren't even twenty, but here in Mongolia they were men. Back in the United States they would still be mostly pampered by their parents.

I remembered that age. I was invincible. Bullet-proof. And while forty wasn't old back home, men my age usually settled for softball and golf, not full-contact sports. Here, people were more philosophical about aging. They embraced it as the next stage in life . . . one to be respected and revered.

When would I have respect for my own age? Was that what Veronica was trying to tell me? Hell, she was in her late twenties. Why would she worry about my age?

I hadn't seen her since she left the stands after Zerleg defeated Dekker. That worried me, but I didn't check up on her, because I assumed Odgerel was in contact. I wanted Ronnie to come to me. I wanted her to say she trusted my judgment and that this was my life to do as I wished. But she hadn't. There wasn't so much as one word from her.

Oh, well. I had pretty much decided it was over anyway, right? There was no way I could reconcile our divergent lives. No, it was better this way. After tomorrow, she'd hop back on a plane to her little ivory tower, thinking of this as just an adventure before settling down in a classroom somewhere.

It saddened me to think this was the only living she would actually do, but it was her decision to make. Just as I owned my life, she owned hers. It was no longer fair for me to judge her or tell her what to do. There. That was mature. Yay, me.

Exhaustion pressed on my chest like a weight. I'd been awake since before dawn. I had wrestled and been broken in both body and soul. The pain I felt emotionally had outstripped the physical pain. Sleep wasn't going to be defeated, and I gave in willingly.

I woke up early the next morning, feeling sore and stiff, but excited by the boys' spirits. Today was the last day of the *naadam*, and it was possible they could win, returning to their families in victory and impressing a girl or two.

I gave them the last of my protein bars and, after

several cups of tea, I started warming them up with exercises. I put on a pair of khaki pants, my *gutals*, a T-shirt and my *deel*, and coached them until Yalta arrived. I saw Ronnie leave with the others to head to the stands. She did not look at me.

We arrived in the stadium, and the boys translated for Yalta and me as we watched the other matches, sizing up the competition. I felt honored that Yalta considered me his assistant. I tried to be helpful and respectful. Zolbin was up soon, and we were watching his opponent warm up.

"Look." I pointed at him for Yalta and spoke in Mongolian. "He favors his left leg. I wonder if he injured his right one yesterday?" Sure enough, as he turned, we saw a large bruise darkening his right calf. Yalta told Zolbin to use his foot to hook him on his sore leg and bring him down. When it was Zolbin's turn, the match lasted all of one minute.

I felt better standing in the sun and being useful. The day's competitors were seasoned, and these bouts took longer. Zerleg barely managed to squeak through his first event, but he won and that was what was important. The boys were scheduled for their second competitions at the same time before noon. Yalta and I split up, and Zerleg and I walked to the opposite end of the field for his match.

"Nervous?" I asked as I stripped off his *deel*.

He was looking anxiously at the stands. "Yes."

I admired the honesty of these people.

"Don't win for Opia," I said. "Win for you." When

I noticed he was still staring at the bleachers, I added, "Or don't win, and you can spend the rest of the day charming her with poetry."

Zerleg laughed at this as the judges indicated they were ready. I stood still as the kid did his eagle dance around me, and it hit me what an honor this was. He considered me his *zazul* and was showing me his respect. I felt a sense of pride others might feel when their son hit a home run or daughter aced that spelling bee. Wow. I didn't see that coming.

The opponents squared off, and I had to stow my feeling of euphoria. It was time to help him from the sidelines. And strangely enough, I really enjoyed it.

"Watch his left arm!" I called. Zerleg didn't have to acknowledge this. I knew he understood. I don't know how I knew, but I did. Zerleg shifted to the right as his opponent tried to sweep his legs using his left arm. The dodge worked. The young men locked their shoulders and began to strain. They appeared evenly matched for strength. Zerleg would have to win on his brains this time.

Chudruk appeared at my side and the two of us continued to shout encouragement. We watched as the two wrestlers moved back and forth, appearing to rock each other. Neither side gave one inch. This was going to be a long match. As Chudruk made suggestions, I realized that all I'd had was one minor glimpse into the world of this sport. There was so much more I would need to devote my life living here to learn. I froze on the spot.

Zerleg went for his opponent's knee. This was the big moment. His competitor somehow managed to step back, saving himself. Zerleg had overestimated his strength and stumbled forward, his right hand catching the ground. It was over.

"You did great, kid." I patted him on the back.

Chudruk smiled at his nephew. "You made us proud!"

Zerleg grinned. It wasn't all about winning here. He had done well. And his prize was a pretty, educated girl beaming at him from the stands. I noticed that as he walked over to her, he didn't even bother to cover up with his *deel*. Tonight he would be celebrating a victory of sorts.

We walked back to the others to find that Zolbin had lost his match too. But Yalta was grinning ear-to-ear. For us, this competition was over. And everyone was happy.

I checked in with the others before heading back to my *ger*. I still had one thing left to do. Dekker would be getting ready to leave. And it was my job to make sure he didn't.

I still didn't have a plan for the hit. Before I formulated one, I'd need to know where Dekker was staying. I really didn't want Veronica to have the answer, but she was the best lead I had at the moment.

"Have you seen Ronnie?" I asked one of Sansar-Huu's children. They were playing in the grass with Sartre.

The girl nodded, then in Mongolian told me that

she had gone east, toward the steppes. I winked and left them to their play.

The campground faded into a large, grassy meadow on the edge of the city. For a moment I wondered if I had misunderstood the kid. I couldn't see anyone. I decided to keep walking for a while before turning back. The grasses were tall, and if Ronnie was sitting on the ground, I'd have a hard time seeing her.

It was the giggling that kept me from turning around and going back. She was here, all right.

"I can't believe you did that! Did you really blow up a plane by accident?" I heard her say.

My blood turned to stone. There was only one person she could be with.

I saw her hair rising above the sea of grass. Then I saw him. Veronica was sitting on a blanket, holding a pen and notebook, while Arje was stretched out on his side next to her. My hands formed fists. I was going to kill him right in front of her.

"Cy!" Veronica jumped a little. That was somewhat satisfying. "What are you doing here?"

Dekker didn't bother getting up. "Bombay," he said gruffly.

"I was told to find you for our interview," I said grimly.

"Oh." Ronnie stared at me, her mind trying to work out when she had said this and to whom.

I sat down and joined them. "Sounds like you've started without me."

"How did Zerleg and Zolbin do?" Ronnie asked,

her voice quavering a little. Did she feel guilty? I wondered how she was going to feel when she watched me rip Dekker's throat out in front of her.

"They both lost." I wasn't interested in making her feel better about playing hooky.

"I'm sorry to hear that," she said quietly, avoiding my eyes.

"I was just telling Ronnie about my work." Dekker's voice had a strange edge. He was challenging me. But for what? Ronnie? Or just that need men had to best an opponent who had taken them down?

I took a deep breath. If I was going to kill him, it had to look like it wasn't premeditated. I replaced my naked fury with a relaxed smile.

"I bet you have some good stories," I said.

Dekker did not relax. You couldn't cut the tension with a Ginsu knife. Ronnie's skin flushed red. It was clear she had never been in a situation like this before.

"Really, guys, this is no big deal. Maybe we can meet up for dinner or something?" She tried to smile but was too nervous. For a moment I allowed myself the luxury of wondering what she was thinking about.

"I don't think Bombay is interested in talking." Dekker's voice was rough . . . ugly with intent. He rose to his feet, fists clenched.

I remained seated but slowly took off my *deel*. It was a gift, after all, and I didn't want it ruined by what was about to happen. I'd been fighting men all of my life. I could spot a gauntlet being thrown down a mile off.

"And why is that?" I asked, feigning innocence.

"I think you know why." He spit the words. There was no mistaking his intent. But where did this come from? Was he fighting because he wanted Ronnie? Or did he know why I was here?

Fighting men have a sixth sense. It is something that has kept them alive on many occasions. The failure to develop this ability means certain death. The sixth sense is one of self-preservation under dangerous circumstances you set in motion yourself. If I survived this, I made a mental note to tell Ronnie so she could use it in her thesis.

Unfortunately, I didn't have much time to think about it, because Dekker charged while I was still on the ground. I would've rolled neatly to the side, but Ronnie was behind me and would bear the brunt of his weight. I lay back, and, using my right arm to shove her away, I brought my feet up and lifted Dekker up and over to the ground behind me.

I was on my feet before he could recover. Ronnie wisely ran off to a safe distance.

"Go back!" I shouted before Dekker charged again. He came at me like a linebacker, his shoulder lowered. Apparently he was going for a "ground and pound" play. I stepped to the left, swiveled and kicked him in the ass.

"Go back!" I shouted at Ronnie again. She just stood there in shock, shaking her head. Great. Now I'd have a witness.

Dekker delivered a roundhouse kick—to my good shoulder, thank God. He'd switched from tackling to kickboxing. I took the blow and landed a side kick to his solar plexus. He stepped backward, regained his balance, then tried a front kick to my right shin. I managed to dodge, hooking his extended leg with mine and twisting him off balance.

Even though I studied it, I'd never really gotten into kickboxing. The idea of fighting on one leg seemed too risky. Now, boxing, there was a sport, I thought, as I landed two jabs with my left and an uppercut with my right to his jaw. Dad was a boxer. It was all about the footwork.

Dekker punched at me, missing my nose but hitting my cheek below my left eye. That was going to look like hell later. I went for a counterblow, but he blocked it. I took advantage of his somewhat doubled-over stance by grabbing the back of his head and bringing my knee up hard into his abdomen. I followed this by bringing my elbow down on the back of his head. He toppled and fell.

"Stop it!" Veronica had found her voice and decided this was a good time to let us know.

It distracted me just enough for Dekker to pull me to the ground. He climbed on top of me and began swinging at my head. Bastard managed to land a few blows. That was what I got for being distracted by a woman.

I punched him in the throat and knocked him off

me. I was just about to get to my feet when he kicked me in the side of the knee, bringing me back down. Great. This was going to take all day.

Why wasn't Veronica running? Didn't it occur to the woman that she could get help? She sure as hell wasn't trying to help me, not that I could blame her with fists and feet flying all over. Still, she needed to go—at the very least so I could kill this bastard once and for all!

I hit the ground hard on my bad shoulder and, in spite of myself, couldn't keep from wincing. Dekker saw that and began a rapid burst of punches to that very same shoulder. How sporting of him.

"Stop hitting him! He's injured!" Ronnie screamed.

Dekker paused long enough for me to see a look of comprehension come over his face. He grinned and drove his elbow into my head. As the stars faded to an inky smear I thought, *At least that solves that mystery.*

Chapter Twenty-two

A desperate disease requires a dangerous remedy.
                                          —GUY FAWKES

"Where's Ronnie!" were the first words out of my mouth as I came to. I wasn't even sure whether I was still in the grass or in a *ger*. Opening my eyes was an exercise in practical pain.

"Quiet, Cy," Odgerel soothed. Other faces swam into view, including my newest BFF, Dr. Baatar.

"Where is she?" I pressed weakly. This time I knew better than to try to get up.

I could see Sansar-Huu look at Chudruk, who looked back at him. That didn't seem good.

"Just be still," Dr. Baatar said quietly.

In spite of the pain, I struggled to move. Why wasn't anyone answering me?

"You have had a second impact to your concussion. You could have brain damage." That caught me up short. The doctor handed me some pills, which I took without question. He spoke in Mongolian to my friends and I gave up even trying to understand them. Instead, I looked around the room. Everyone was there. Well, almost everyone.

"You have to rest. The doctor did not see any signs

of damage, but you can't leave here tonight," Sansar-Huu said once Dr. Baatar had gone. "He will be back in the morning. You may need to go to the hospital for a CT scan."

"All right. Fine. Just tell me where Ronnie is and I promise I will rest."

"She came and told us where you were, and then she left," Zerleg said.

"We haven't seen her since," Zolbin added.

I struggled to get up. "I have to find her. . . ."

"Cy!" Odgerel shouted. "You cannot go anywhere. Ronnie will be fine. Just tell us what happened."

I hated to admit it, but I wouldn't be of help to anyone in this condition. I slowly lowered myself back down and filled everyone in on the fight.

"I'm afraid Ronnie's gone after Dekker," I finished.

"Why?" Chudruk asked.

"I don't know. To chew him out. To ask him why." My words were starting to spin around in my mouth and they tasted sour.

Sansar-Huu, Chudruk, Zerleg and Zolbin took off immediately to search the campground. Odgerel and Yalta insisted on staying with me. I watched as my *zazul* took a chair outside to sit and keep watch. I felt sorry for Dekker if he came back to finish me off.

"She has feelings for you, you know," Odgerel said as she put a cold cloth on my head.

"Does she?" Deep down I knew she was right. I just had a hard time believing it.

"Yes. And you have feelings for her."

I didn't say anything. I was too worried about Ronnie. Why did she run off like that? What could she have been thinking?

"Veronica was very upset when she came here to tell us you were hurt," Odgerel continued.

"It wasn't her fault," I said.

She looked at me, puzzled. "What do you mean?"

So I explained my jealousy over Dekker's flirting with her and how Ronnie knew all about it.

"I was an ass," I concluded.

My friend laughed. "Yes! You were!" She went off to admonish the kids, who were laughing at something. A second later she placed Sartre on my chest. As I started to stroke her fur, she purred. And it seemed I was back to where I'd started.

It was kind of soothing lying on the cot, petting my pig while the kids played on the floor. Odgerel sang songs that made the children giggle as she went about the preparations for dinner. I tried to think about what I needed to do to kill Dekker, but my head hurt too much. The pills the doctor gave me helped a little, but did nothing for the fear I had for Ronnie.

Sartre slid down into my armpit, snuggled up and went to sleep. That was soothing. A couple of times the kids tried to snatch her up, but their mother was always there to step in. I tried not to think of what Dekker might do to Veronica. So I tried to imagine that I was in my own *ger* with Veronica. What would our children be like?

That may have been the first time I ever thought

about having kids with anyone. Oh, I loved kids. My cousins had some really funny children. I just never wanted any of my own. Most of the women I messed around with already had families. It just never came up. Part of the reason was that once the kids turned five, they had to start school. My life wasn't meant for settling down and joining the PTA. And at five, Bombay kids had to start their training.

I supposed with our combined educations Veronica and I could homeschool as we traveled. Although I didn't think my wife would like me training our children to become hired killers. What strange thoughts went through your head when you'd been clubbed by a Dutch mercenary at a Mongolian wrestling festival.

Zerleg and Zolbin burst through the door, rudely awakening Sartre. She let them know her displeasure with a loud, "Wheek," then set about chewing on my T-shirt.

"We can't find her!" Zerleg said, out of breath.

"We looked everywhere!" Zolbin panted.

Within the hour, Sansar-Huu and Chudruk returned with similar information.

"Two men I know saw her leave the grounds with Dekker," Chudruk added.

It was silent in the *ger* for a few moments. I handed the guinea pig off to the children and they immediately fattened her up with grass.

"Why would she go with him?" Zolbin asked. His uncle shot him a look. It occurred to me that everyone here thought Veronica had chosen Dekker over me.

They didn't know what kind of man he was, what kind of danger Ronnie was in.

"I think I need to tell you a little something about Arje Dekker. Odgerel, could you send the kids outside for a few moments?"

Yalta came in when the kids went out. Chudruk translated. I told them I'd met Dekker on the circuit and read about him in the news. This seemed to mollify my friends. When I told them about the atrocities he'd committed, they were horrified. These were the descendants of the great Genghis Khan. They knew about the horrors of war. But the brutality of what Dekker had done shocked them.

"I don't know why he has targeted me, and I don't care. What I do care about is making sure he doesn't hurt Veronica to get my attention."

I had just finished when there was a knock at the door. Sansar-Huu's oldest poked her head in and handed Zolbin a note.

"She says a boy dropped this off." He handed the note to me.

My name was on the outside. The eyes of everyone in the tent were on me as I opened it.

Meet me at the abandoned block of flats outside of the city.

He included directions. How thoughtful. But what time? And would he have Veronica with him? He didn't say to come alone.

177

I looked around the room. There was no way I could involve my friends in this. But I would need a ride.

Sansar-Huu turned off the headlights and coasted into a crumbling parking lot. It was almost midnight. And very dark. I felt for the flashlight in my pocket.

"We will look around for Veronica," he whispered, pointing at Chudruk.

"Just stay out of sight. I'll yell when it's over," I replied. This time I was taking no chances. Chudruk had given me his set of throwing knives—a sport I'd taught him when we worked together in the States. My goal was to find Dekker so my friends could find Veronica. We were a block from the meeting site.

Dekker had chosen a pile of rubble that used to be a Soviet-designed apartment building. There were many places he could hide. This was the perfect location for an ambush. Whatever happened, it had to be quick and quiet. I wanted this man dead once and for all.

My friends would go on foot around the perimeter, carefully searching for Ronnie. Both men were armed with old semiautomatics. We only had two guns, and I thought it would be better if they carried them. I could work quickly with knives.

My plan was to walk into the middle of the complex. Dekker wanted to see me. Well, that was what he was going to get. I waited until my eyes adjusted to the darkness. Then I headed in.

The air was sharp, in spite of its being July. I heard the clinking of broken cement on twisted, exposed rebar as rats slithered in the darkness. I wanted to find him right away. I was going to kill Arje Dekker if I had to do it with my bare hands. Fortunately, I could do that. It was simple leverage, really.

I heard footsteps off to my left. They were moving quickly in my direction, so I ducked into a broken entryway. The darkness smothered all light. The steps grew louder and I tightened my grip on one of the knives. Suddenly, the footsteps stopped, then started running in the opposite direction.

Lunging from my doorway, I flipped on my flashlight, only to see a shadow ahead round the corner. I was so busy concentrating on what was in front of me, I failed to look down. Something large tripped me. I fell, immediately twisting to my right. Pulling out the knife, I hurled myself at the body. It didn't move.

I shined the flashlight and found the unconscious form of Veronica Gale on the ground in front of me. This left me with a dilemma: I could run after Dekker, or get this woman to safety. This wasn't her fight. She wasn't supposed to be here. The choice was clear.

I carried her back to the truck over my good shoulder and placed her gently in the passenger seat. I started the car and drove to the ruins, honking the horn again and again. Chudruk and Sansar-Huu emerged from the darkness and climbed in.

"He drove off." Chudruk pointed toward the airport.

"She's bleeding," Sansar-Huu said. "She's been hit in the head. Her breathing is shallow."

I wasn't even surprised to see Dr. Baatar at the hospital. He admitted Veronica and me, giving us both CT scans and thoroughly checking us out. He assigned us to a room for the night, and Chudruk stayed to stand guard while Sansar-Huu went back to the *ger*. I passed out once the doctor convinced me Ronnie was all right. I slept like a stone.

Chapter Twenty-three

Evey Hammond: [*reads*] Vi Veri Veniversum Vivus
   Vici.
V: [*translates*] By the power of truth, I, while living,
   have conquered the universe.
Evey Hammond: Personal motto?
V: From *Faust*.
Evey Hammond: That's about trying to cheat the
   devil, isn't it?
V: It is.

—*V FOR VENDETTA*

I'd been around a lot of dirtbags in my life. And I'd
gotten to kill most of them. But none of them had ever
been a real threat to me before. Maybe partly because
I'd been younger, but mostly because I had been unattached. Bad guys had no leverage, nothing to threaten
me with that would actually scare me in any way. Some
of my cousins had been through rough times with
either their kids being kidnapped or the people they
loved threatened in some way. But not me.

   This was new. Veronica was in danger. Because of
me. And my vic had escaped his sentence because of
my mistakes. This was unheard-of. I didn't think

anyone in the Bombay tribe had ever had to chase a vic. We always took them out where they stood.

My confidence, for the first time in my life, was shaken. I couldn't just walk away from this one. And I didn't know what to do. My number one task was to hunt down Arje Dekker and kill him so that Veronica was safe.

"Uh . . ." Veronica shifted on the hospital bed.

"Veronica?" I asked gently, closing the gap between our beds.

"Cy?" She looked up at me and frowned, then closed her eyes.

"You're all right. The doctor says you are fine. We're booked on the next flight home." There was no reaction. But even if she was unconscious, it made me feel good to tell her that she was safe. Of course, I left out that the next flight home was on the Bombay family's private plane, but I figured she didn't need to hear that.

My biggest concern was Dekker. He was gone, and I was convinced that he knew that I was going to kill him. And I would kill him. There was no doubt about that.

Chudruk and Sansar-Huu went back to get Veronica's and my things. I stepped out of the room to make a phone call.

"Missi?" I said quietly as my cousin answered. "I'm going to need the family jet and some information on Dekker's whereabouts."

"Hey, Coney!" came a voice that was not Missi's. "It's Monty. Mom's on assignment."

Damn. I really needed her. She was the one person who could get me what I needed. Leave it to the Bombay Council to send her out when she was our best techie.

"The jet will be there tomorrow morning." Monty's voice interrupted my thoughts. "Who's Dekker?"

Montgomery Bombay was one of Missi's twin teenage sons. "Look, Monty, I appreciate the help. But you don't have the chops yet to—"

"Okay, got it. Arje Dekker, on a flight to Berlin, then on to London. I can have you two land at Heathrow at the same time."

"Um, okay." You know, I shouldn't be surprised by anything that happens in this family.

Monty sighed on the other end. "I just hacked into the system. It's not like it was *hard*."

"Sorry, kid. I underestimated you."

"And I'm not a kid. You guys should figure that out. Mom trained me. "

"Sorry, Monty." And I meant it. Underestimating any Bombay was a dangerous venture. "So what's my ETA in London?"

A few minutes later I hung up with everything I needed to know.

By the time Chudruk and the boys showed up, Ronnie was sitting up and eating. An hour later, she was moving around the room. She made it clear that she didn't want to talk about what had happened. I could give her that. But once we got on the plane, I would have to know. Which meant I would also have to give her some insight into who Dekker was.

We slept hard that night. And in the morning Sansar-Huu and the others met us with the pickup and all of our gear.

"Thanks, Chudruk." I hugged my friend and shook hands with Zerleg, Zolbin and Yalta. I would truly miss them.

"It has been good to see you." Chudruk smiled.

I turned to Zerleg and held out a slip of paper. "The dean at Yale is a good friend of mine. He owes me money. He is expecting your call."

Zerleg looked at me, then at his uncle. He took the paper with a nod and flung his arms around me.

"You have a full scholarship, if you want it," I wheezed as the boy crushed me to him. I didn't tell him that the scholarship was from the Bombay Trust I had established at the Ivy League school. He didn't really need to know that.

Veronica stared at me, but said nothing. She continued her silence as we made our way to the airport and onto our private jet. It wasn't until we were seated and I pulled Sartre out that she finally spoke.

"You have a private jet? And how did you get Zerleg into Yale?"

"Ah. She speaks. There must be intelligent life in that body after all."

Sartre sank her teeth into my finger. Apparently she was on Ronnie's side.

"Don't give me that crap, Cy." She gripped the armrests as the plane taxied down the runway. "When are you going to tell me who you really are?"

I gave her a look. "Who I really am? You mean I still don't fit neatly into one of your stereotypes?"

"I'm not sure you're even human!" she shouted. "How is this possible? How does a carney have a private plane at his beck and call?"

I pulled a carrot out of my pocket and gave it to the guinea pig on my lap. She took it as if she were the queen of Sheba and deserved such things.

"My family owns this jet. We are independently wealthy."

Ronnie sat back and chewed her lip. "I guess that explains how you got into Yale and your connections for Zerleg."

"Don't piss me off, Veronica. I got into Yale because of my brains. My family doesn't believe in undue influence over things like that." And that was sort of true. Undue influence to get your kid into a good school . . . no. Undue influence to use the CIA to bail your kid out of a minor skirmish in Botswana . . . yes. It just depended on how you looked at it.

"Right." She rolled her eyes.

"You said you don't know who I really am," I said calmly. "What did you mean by that?"

Veronica chewed her lip. Something was up.

"Did Dekker say something to you?"

She nodded. "He told me I really didn't know you. Who you are. What you are."

Well, that stopped me in my tracks. What did Dekker know about me? I was off the grid. Hell, I didn't even have a social security number.

"Oh, yes," I said quietly. "You should definitely take the word of a man who kidnapped you and dumped you unconscious in the worst part of town."

She threw her hand up into the air. "What is it with you men anyway? How in the hell did I end up in this weird situation? I was perfectly happy in my little apartment at the university. But now I'm on a carney's private jet after being kidnapped by some Dutch wrestler in Mongolia!"

"That is a lot to think about. Maybe you're bad at decision making?" I teased.

"The only bad decision I made was to think I had feelings for you, Coney Bombay!"

Now, that hurt.

Chapter Twenty-four

"The illegal, we do immediately. The unconstitutional takes a little longer."

—HENRY KISSINGER

Luisa, the family's staff on the Bombay private plane, interrupted us with plates of pastries and cups of tea. She smiled at me, touching me briefly on the shoulder before returning to her suite at the rear of the jet. She'd been with us for years, replacing her mother, Inez, who had worked with us since the 1950s. Luisa was petite and gorgeous, with a knockout grin and a sharp mind. She was only twenty-five, and most of my cousins had hit on her from time to time—with no success whatsoever. I never did. Maybe that was why she always flirted with me.

"And who was that?" Veronica asked, her voice a bit strained.

"That is Luisa," I answered, sipping my tea. It was Darjeeling. My favorite.

"She's a bit forward, isn't she?" The jealousy she was trying so hard not to show was adorable.

"She likes me." Why should I tell Veronica that Luisa and I were just associates? She wasn't giving me anything on Dekker.

"Is she one of your carney groupies?" The words had a sharp edge to them.

"No."

Veronica crossed her arms over her chest and fumed in silence for a moment. I took the opportunity to eat and drink.

The silence was tense, but I needed it to figure a few things out. First of all, what was I going to do with Ronnie? She would have to go home so I could continue to pursue Dekker. Maybe she'd take Sartre with her. That would give me an excuse to look her up when this assignment was over.

And what did Dekker mean when he said he knew who I was? I was a carney, a drifter, totally forgettable to most people. What could he know? The Bombay family of assassins had been a closely guarded secret since 2000 BCE. There was no way any vic could know about us.

Then again, a man like Dekker had many, many enemies. It made sense that he would guess there was a contract out on him, even if he didn't necessarily know exactly who was targeting him.

Because of his contact with Veronica, he knew my name. He knew I was a Bombay. A chill slid down my spine. He could get to my family. That was bad. Very bad. I pulled out my cell phone and texted Monty. Within minutes he replied with an expletive I was pretty sure his mother didn't let him use.

"Isn't it dangerous to use a cell phone on a plane?" Veronica asked.

"No," I answered, slipping the phone into my pocket.

"Aren't you interfering with the plane's guidance system or something?"

"No. It has nothing to do with that."

"Why not?"

I turned to look at her. "The real reason they don't want you to use cells on a plane is because you might crash the cell phone service by taking up too much of the power from towers on the land."

She smirked. "And yours won't?"

"No. Mine is special."

Sartre squeaked and lunged off my lap toward Veronica. Ronnie responded by taking the little pig into her arms. Traitor.

"When we get to London, I'm getting off. The pilot will take you to your nearest airport. Will you take Sartre with you?"

She frowned. "You want me to go home? What are you going to do in London?"

"Take care of some business. I'll pick up Sartre when I'm done."

Ronnie shook her head. "No. I'm going with you."

"What? No. You aren't." I hadn't anticipated this reaction. I thought she'd just want to get as far away as possible. At least from me.

"You are going after Arje, aren't you?"

"That's between me and him, Veronica."

She snorted. "Oh, yeah. I wasn't involved at all."

I thought about this. She was right. But I didn't

want her to get hurt again. And I needed time to sort out my feelings . . . without her around.

"I'm not going home, Cy," she said firmly. "That's the deal."

"This isn't your fight," I replied. "He hurt you to get to me."

"Then how do you know I'll be safe back home?"

She was right. The safest place for Veronica Gale was with me. But I didn't want her to be there when I killed him.

"And you are not backing out on your promise."

My eyebrows went up. "My promise?"

She nodded smugly. "You said you'd help me solve Senator Anderson's murder."

Shit. I did. Didn't I? "I can do that once I've taken care of Dekker."

"And just what does 'taken care of' mean, anyway? Are you going to kill him?"

Veronica's words vibrated through me. She hit too close to home. Did she think I was going to kill him?

"What did Arje Dekker tell you about me?"

She looked uncertain. "He said you were hired to kill him. Is that true?"

"No." *Yes.*

Her shoulders relaxed. "Who is he? And why did he attack you like that?"

It kind of warmed my heart a bit that she was more concerned about him hurting me than him hurting her.

"He's a mercenary. The worst kind. A mass murderer on a global scale."

Ronnie looked shaken. "What do you mean?"

So I told her. I told her everything about the nice Dutchman she thought was so cute. And I left nothing to the imagination. She deserved to know the truth. And yes, I wanted her to hate him. Sue me.

"Oh, my God," Veronica whispered when I was through. "I . . . I had no idea."

"I'm sorry, Ronnie." And I was. "But now you know you can't stay with me. A man like that will kill you next time. He's just not the sentimental type."

"Why don't you call Interpol or something? Why do you need to go after him?"

Good question. Too good. I had no answer. What was I going to say?

"Do you think someone like him was responsible for Anderson's murder?"

"What?" I hadn't expected that response. "Ronnie, there's no evidence Anderson was murdered."

She actually unbuckled her seat belt and stood. "You said you would help me. You promised." Veronica wavered a little unsteadily on her feet. Maybe she'd left the hospital too soon. I led her over to a divan and forced her to lie down.

"And I will. But you have to realize that one of the possibilities is that Anderson died of a heart attack."

She nodded, but it was only a physical agreement. Her eyes told another story.

"Look, we have a few hours. Let's go over what you have." Then I could make good on my promise *and* change the subject. Maybe by the time we landed at Heathrow I could convince her to go home and drop this case. A two-for-one deal, if you will.

Veronica's file on Senator Anderson was three inches thick. And because she had the time, she had managed to review more than one hundred and sixty-two suspects. These suspects had, at one time or another, threatened the senator. Unfortunately, she included in with the serious threats people who had threatened to have city hall nab him for not mowing his grass, two pastors, a thirteen-year-old paper boy and a conservative talk-show host.

"Okay. Let's narrow this down a bit," I began. "I mean, do you really think Oprah's hairstylist wanted to kill a senator?"

"Yeah, I know." Ronnie sighed and brushed a strand of hair from her face. "I guess I went a little crazy. Then again, the woman did make his hair look ridiculous. But I see where you're going with this."

"There has to be a motive for murder. And I'm still not convinced it was anything more than a bad heart." I held up two medical forms. "How in the hell did you get these?" Wasn't anything confidential anymore?

"From another theorist."

"Well, they prove that the man had a rotten ticker. And there's a lot of stress in holding public office."

"I know that, but something about the whole thing just doesn't feel right. You know?"

"Fine. Let's go through these names, then."

The rest of the flight went quickly as we went through each name on her extensive list. Veronica was willing to concede that Anderson's elderly kindergarten teacher and his neighbors weren't proper suspects. I had to admit, her notes were pretty thorough. Anderson did have a lot of enemies. There were a lot of people who felt he was too revolutionary in his ideas.

"All right. So we have it narrowed down to four people, and you have excellent penmanship." I stretched my arms above my head. The shoulder was starting to heal now that I wasn't taking a beating every day. "But I think your research is pretty one-sided."

Veronica was making piles from the pages we sorted. "How so?"

"Well, you only have information from major newspapers, liberal magazines and networks here. What about alternative papers, independent radio, the international press?"

"Well, I admit I haven't really gone that far." She looked tired and more than a little concerned. I suppose I could've given her a hard time about the basic tenets of scholarly research, but I just couldn't do it. She'd been through too much.

I pulled her close and silently held her in my arms until the plane landed.

Chapter Twenty-five

Emperor Zhark: What's the point in possessing a devastatingly destructive death ray if you can't use it?

—*THE WELL OF LOST PLOTS*, JASPER FFORDE

London. One of my favorite cities. I did some postgraduate work once upon a time there and loved it ever since. It was a city where history came alive and grappled with itself. I still had some valuable contacts there. And it gave me an idea.

"Who are you calling?" Veronica asked.

"A friend who can help you." *And hopefully take you off my hands and keep you safe while I flush out my vic.*

A few minutes later, I was hustling Ronnie through the airport toward the baggage claim.

"Richard works for the *Sentinel*. It's the largest independent paper in the world, and it can give you a more unbiased perspective," I said as I hailed a taxi.

"He's waiting for you at the door." I told the driver where to take Veronica, and to see that she got there safely I threw in one hundred euros. "I'll meet up with you later."

Ronnie looked at me in a way that said she wasn't sure about this idea. But I was. And I could feel it as I shut the door on her and smacked the cab, sending it on its way.

"Monty," I said into the Bluetooth I'd just inserted. "Where is Vic?"

"Hey, Coney! It's Jack!" Missi's other twin greeted me on the phone. Great, now I'd have to explain what I was doing all over again.

"We've been following him on the airport security cameras ever since the plane landed. He's in the shopping area," Jack said before I could reply. "Did you know Mom's a contestant on a reality show?"

"I heard that," I said quickly as I made my way through the terminal. "Where in the shopping area?"

"Looks like a toy store or something. It's hard to tell . . . Hold on. I'll find out what toy stores are there and map it for you on the phone," Jack said, and within seconds I could see a little red dot indicating Dekker's position. It looked as though he was in a room about two hundred yards on my right.

"Keep it on until I make visual confirmation."

"Roger that," Jack answered. I was pretty impressed with the boys. I made a mental note to knit that bag Missi wanted using the cashmere I'd gotten from Mongolia.

It should be said that it isn't easy walking fast without looking like you are walking fast. There really is only one place where everyone moves that way. And that is an airport. As I closed in on the location, I congratulated myself for getting rid of Ronnie and fulfilling my promise to her at the same time.

"You should be within range now." Jackson's voice rang in my ear. Oh, yeah, the assignment.

"I see it," I answered. Dekker was standing with his back to me. Apparently he didn't think I would catch up to him. That was his fault for underestimating technology in a place as security conscious as an international airport.

I suppose I could have said something clever or tapped him on the shoulder to get his attention. That's what they do in movies. But that's not how it is done in real life. I came up behind him and grabbed him by the neck. Forcing his head down I managed to make it connect with the table full of stuffed badgers in front of him.

Unfortunately for me, the table had stuffed badgers on it and I wasn't able to stun him. Arje Dekker pushed up and back, shoving me into a display of fluffy bunnies. By the time I steadied myself, he'd turned around and realized who I was.

"Bombay!" Dekker cried, and reached for something to throw at me.

I stood there in shock as a Slinky collided with my forehead. My hands felt around me and grasped something square and plastic. I whipped the Etch A Sketch at his head, the tablet careening off his chin. As he recovered from the blow, I grabbed him by the lapels and dragged him deeper into the store. I hoped there would be a back door somewhere, since I noticed we were drawing a small crowd.

Dekker kicked out, connecting with my left shin,

and I dropped him for a second. That was all the time he needed to grab a weapon. Without thinking I pulled a similar item from a box. And that was how we ended up fighting a duel with plastic lightsabers.

We must have looked strange—two middle-aged men slashing away at each other with toy swords complete with sound effects. I managed to land the majority of blows and went for the final thrust, only to have the collapsible lightsaber, um, collapse. So I threw the handle at him and grabbed him again, dragging him toward the back wall.

Dekker reached out and snagged a display case. I threw him through it, causing no less than thirty or forty Teletubbies to begin singing nonsensically. By now I was getting worried. The shop probably had surveillance cameras, and we'd put on quite a show. In fact, I'd bet Jackson was laughing hysterically. I was a bit surprised none of the staff intervened or even rebuked us. No doubt airport security had been called.

I pulled Dekker by the collar toward the back door. It was a bathroom. No exit. Dekker shoved me backward and locked himself inside. Fantastic.

There was shouting in the distance. The authorities were on their way. Killing Vic was out of the question.

"Jack, can you do something about the surveillance cameras?" I asked quietly while taking off my jacket, and started messing with the doorknob. It was a simple lock, easy to pick if I had the right tools.

"Already did. They have nothing but static," he responded. "It's a neat little program Mom came up with. . . ."

The boy was chatty, just like his mom. "Thanks, Jack. I'll check in with you later." I hung up, quickly found a chemistry set back at the toy store and punched through the box. Science kits usually have probes and other tools you can use to pick a lock. Unfortunately, the box had that plastic clamshell casing that keeps everything pretty and safe inside. I didn't have time for this frustration. Ignoring the sharp edges that tore at my flesh, I ripped the plastic apart and retrieved the tools.

I managed to get the door open quickly and dragged Dekker out of the bathroom and into the mall. It wasn't easy to look normal when you were bleeding and dragging a man behind you (who clearly had no interest in going with you) who was also bleeding. It wouldn't be long before we attracted enough attention to cause trouble. And I didn't have time for that. If I took him to the plane I could secure him and go after Ronnie. But the hangar was too far away. I was much closer to the baggage carousel.

Pulling my protesting vic behind me, I stepped outside and hailed a cab. To his credit, the driver didn't give my situation a second glance, and soon we were headed to the newspaper where Ronnie was researching.

The ride was short, but I had enough time to bind Dekker's hands with his own belt. The cab pulled up to our stop and I paid him and dragged Dekker out and into the building.

We'd just entered the elevator when I realized my vic was apparently quite the Houdini. As the doors closed, he broke his bonds and lunged. I swung my arm up and stepped aside, clotheslining him in the throat. He didn't go down like I'd hoped.

"You don't give up, do you?" Dekker growled as he punched me in the head.

"Don't know the meaning of the word," I replied, kneeing him in the gut.

And as the Muzak played "The Girl from Ipanema," Dekker and I pounded the hell out of each other in a three-foot-by-three-foot lift. Arje remembered my weak spots and was getting the best of me with several punches to my shoulder. I managed to crack his nose. The snapping sound made me feel a little better.

Soon the linoleum was slick with blood. Dekker leaned for a side kick and succeeded in plunging his foot through a hole in the wall he created. I punched him in the groin and took a lot of satisfaction in his cry of pain. I hadn't even noticed that the elevator had stopped until we both fell forward through the open doors.

"Cy? Arje?" Veronica said as she stood over us.

Ronnie?

Before Dekker could react I slugged him hard on the chin, driving his head back and rendering him unconscious. "Stay where you are. I've got to get him out of here."

Veronica stared, wide eyed.

Somehow I managed to rise to my feet and drag Dekker across the hall to a bathroom. What was it with me and bathrooms lately? I handed Veronica a few paper towels and asked her to clean up the bloody smear trailing down the hall. She didn't say a word.

Ronnie joined me in the small bathroom a few minutes later with red-stained paper towels. I locked the door behind her, leaning against it to catch my breath.

"So, this is the *Sentinel*'s office," I gasped as nonchalantly as possible.

"Yup."

I made my way to the sink and started washing up. "I'm sorry to cut short your research, but we have to leave. Now."

Veronica looked pale. She shrugged.

Somehow I had to kill him in front of her. If I didn't, he would continue tracking her down. And I couldn't have that either.

"Um, I . . ." She started, but couldn't seem to finish. "Why did you two end up here?"

I shook my head. "No time to explain. He's dangerous, Ronnie." I hoped she caught my meaning.

"Can't we just call the police or something? Then they could lock him up—"

"No. If he wants to, he'll have no problem hunting you down anywhere. This ends now." On the outside, I was calm. On the inside I was shaking. I'd never killed anyone in the presence of a non-Bombay before. And I was pretty sure that would spell the end of my relationship with Miss Gale.

Ronnie pulled on my arm. "Let's go! Let's just go!"

I avoided looking into her eyes. I didn't want to see what I thought was in there. It made me sick inside to even consider killing Dekker in front of her.

Looking down at the unconscious and bloody man before me, I realized that there was only one way to handle this. And it might have been my worst idea ever.

Chapter Twenty-six

Bob Wiley: What are you doing with the gun, Dr. Marvin?
Dr. Leo Marvin: Death Therapy, Bob. It's a guaranteed cure.

—*What About Bob?*

The idea of doing a good job is instilled in every Bombay from the minute we begin our training at the age of five. We are taught to make sure each assignment is completed with no screwups. Every Bombay has their own modus operandi. And every one of us takes pride in completing the assignment in a timely manner.

We found the freight elevator in the back, and we were able to at least make it to the ground floor undetected. The doors opened, and I spotted a janitor's closet. It took two extra-large garbage bags to cover the unconscious vic. Ronnie convinced me to poke holes in the bag around his face so he wouldn't suffocate. That was too bad, because I was hoping I could tell her I "accidentally" asphyxiated him.

I sent Veronica to find a cab, and she showed up with my former driver. I guess the guy liked the three-figure tip I gave him. He said nothing as I loaded Vic's body into his trunk.

"Your hands are bleeding." Ronnie took my hands in hers and examined the torn-up knuckles. "You got that from . . ." Her eyes darted between the driver in front of us and the trunk behind us. "From the elevator?"

I shook my head. "No. They got torn up while I was trying to open a toy."

"I hate those things!" The driver spoke up with a grin in the rearview window. "It should be criminal to make the plastic covers for toys!"

I gave him a nod that hopefully conveyed something like, *Yeah, me too. Stop talking to us.* He seemed to take the hint and focused on getting us back to the airport. I'd texted the pilot, and he found us an alternative way in so we wouldn't have to go through security checkpoints.

"Well, I hope they have some bandages on the plane," Veronica said quietly as she continued inspecting my wounds. "You could get a serious infection."

I didn't say anything. Frankly, I was wiped out. Dekker was far too dangerous to be dragged around alive. But Ronnie wouldn't let me kill him. Oh, sure, I could just off him anyway. That was what I would've done pre–Veronica Gale. I couldn't do it. I couldn't kill him with her right here. It was just too complicated.

So how it came to pass that Arje Dekker was tied up in one of the family jet's bathrooms was still unsettling even after we took off.

"Sorry, Cy," Veronica apologized for the eleventh time since we'd smuggled him on board. "We'll come up with what to do with him."

I ran my hands through my hair. Yes, I supposed she was right. I had no clue how to manage it, but oh, well.

"How did your research go?" I asked in an effort to change the subject.

"Well," Ronnie started. "I found some information. Richard was very helpful."

"Are you stalling?"

"No." But the way she looked nervously from side to side said otherwise.

"Then what did you find out?" I reached for the files she'd been carrying in her bag. She handed them to me hesitantly.

The look on her face made me pause. "Would you rather tell me or let me read it for myself?"

Ronnie shook her head slowly. "I'll tell you. It's just that . . . well, I found something out that kind of upset me."

It's always a shock when your heroes fall. It's even harder to watch the face of someone you care about when they realize what they believe is a lie.

"Senator Anderson was involved with a couple of women who weren't his wife." She fidgeted with her hair.

"Okay."

"He *apparently*"—I noted how she said the word, as if saying it that way would make it less true—"was involved with a couple of prostitutes from the same escort service."

My heart wrenched as she held out two photos. I

knew this was hard for her. The pictures revealed a man in flagrante delicto with two women at the same time. While I was impressed, I thought it wouldn't be wise to say so.

"I guess he wasn't all I thought he was," Veronica said finally.

With a sigh I gathered her into my arms. Something inside me begged me never to disappoint her like Anderson had.

"Nobody's perfect, Ronnie," I said softly as she pulled away. Why was she pulling away?

"I thought he was. I thought he was perfect. Why didn't these photos run in the United States?"

"It's hard to say. The media isn't always as objective as we'd like them to be."

"And if I didn't know about this after all my research, what else didn't I know?" Her calm voice quavered, betraying the agony beneath her words.

"Probably a lot." I had some strong opinions here but decided this wasn't the time to bring it up. The fact is that many politicians are corrupt or crooked or easily seduced. Usually sexual deviances are just the tip of the iceberg. I was a bit irritated that Veronica had put this man on a pedestal in the first place.

"You don't understand, Cy." She dropped her head into her hands. "This guy and his volunteers were my family when I didn't have one."

"I can understand that. But the fact that you are in education should tell you that things aren't always what they seem. You've learned to look at people and ideas from all sides before drawing conclusions." Right? She had to do that. It was part of the core of knowledge. Critical thinking meant you didn't hedge your bets.

"You mean like what I thought about you?" She motioned toward the back of the plane. "Or Dekker? Yeah. I've been really good at drawing conclusions."

When dealing with women, you have to tread carefully. Somehow I expected this was one case where she wouldn't necessarily want me to agree. Then again, if I sugarcoated the truth, how was I helping her learn?

"But you know better now," I replied.

She looked up sharply, fire in her eyes. I knew it. There was no right way to play this one.

Veronica stood and stalked toward the back of the plane, then plunked herself in a chair by the window.

Okay, that conversation was done. I wasn't going to follow her back and smooth things over. She was wrong. She even admitted it. How mature to throw a fit like that.

Besides, I had other problems. One was trussed up like a Thanksgiving turkey in the bathroom. And the problem was that he was still breathing. Not good.

Maybe I needed to cut Veronica Gale loose once and for all. Just drop her off at her precious university while she still believed that Anderson's only sins were sexual. It had been a mistake to send her to the newspaper. What was I thinking? This kid had one hero—one! And I imposed my will to make her see what a fool she was.

And yes, she'd been wrong about me. But why did I care? Lots of people had misconceptions about Coney Island Bombay. I never cared before. And it wasn't like I wanted her to know what I really was. So why did I want her to see me differently?

I got up and moved past the sulking Ronnie toward the tiny bathroom where Dekker was.

"Hello, Arje," I said as I closed the door and sat down on the toilet seat.

Dekker glared but said nothing. Mainly this was because of the duct tape covering his mouth. He was pissed off, but it didn't matter. I had him tied up pretty well. So what made me reach over and rip the tape off of his face?

"So, you probably know you are going to die," I said as simply as I could.

"But I'm not dead yet, Bombay. Why is that, I wonder?"

"You can thank Ronnie for that. She gets a little freaked out by violence."

Dekker grinned. "Yeah. Funny how she ended up around us."

I toyed with asking him what he thought he knew about me, but changed my mind. "What is it with women anyway? Why do they question our need for fighting?"

Arje looked at the door, then at me. "I don't know. Never really had a relationship with anyone other than whores. And they were paid to keep their mouths shut. But I know what you're saying."

I leaned back against the wall. "I like fighting. I enjoy competing. I know it's barbaric." And I did too.

Dekker sighed. "And I like war."

I looked up at him. "Yes, but you also like killing innocents along with soldiers."

He nodded. "You've heard the rumors, then. I'm surprised someone like you would believe everything you read."

"What the hell is that supposed to mean?" I growled.

"I just expected more from you, that's all."

"So you are saying that you don't kill innocent people? I guess you are just misunderstood."

"No, I'm not saying that, Bombay," Dekker said slowly. "You of all people should know that sometimes bad things happen to good people. It's the nature of war."

I let his words chill me for a moment. He was right. No matter how careful or just any war was, sometimes innocent people got killed. But I wasn't going to give him the satisfaction.

"The way I hear it, and my sources are good, *you*"—I pointed at him directly—"don't seem to mind it when an unarmed woman or child gets in the way."

Dekker's face darkened with something I couldn't read. "Believe what you want." He turned his face away, indicating the conversation was over.

I replaced the duct tape over his mouth. "That's right. I remember why I'm going to kill you." As I stood up, I paused. "Thanks, Dekker."

What the hell was I thinking, talking to him like that? Man, Veronica Gale was really messing with my head. I needed to get rid of her, then get rid of Dekker, find my RV and immerse myself in carnival sawdust and stale corn dogs.

Chapter Twenty-seven

Longbaugh: A heart is the only thing that has value.
 If you have one, get rid of it.
 —*THE WAY OF THE GUN*

We landed at the Cedar Rapids, Iowa, airport several hours later. The pilot would get the plane refueled by the time I returned for Dekker. I'd like to say that, as the plane taxied to a halt, Veronica and I made up and had sex the entire time. I'd like to say that. But I can't. We barely spoke. I don't know why I was being so stubborn about this. But then, she was being stubborn too.

The saying *Two wrongs don't make a right* popped into my head. I ignored it as I rented a car and loaded Ronnie's things into the trunk. We drove in silence to Iowa City. It was an unbearable twenty minutes. I decided I'd take her home, then get rid of Vic and go home myself.

The only time she spoke was to give me directions to her apartment. We pulled up in front of a Victorian house with a wraparound porch. To my complete surprise, a very attractive young man about Ronnie's age came out the front door and hugged her. Who in the hell was that?

"Hi." The guy came up to me and shook my hand. "I'm Drew. Thanks for bringing Veronica home."

Home? Home was with this guy? Whoa. What was going on here? I looked at Ronnie. She stood there with her hands on her hips. What did that mean?

I shook his hand, trying to control my temper. "Cy Bombay. And it's no problem. She's all yours." I shot a look at Ronnie, who threw her hands up in the air while Drew grabbed her luggage.

"You failed to mention Drew," I said evenly.

She grinned. "I guess you can't pigeonhole me either."

"What is that supposed to mean?"

"You don't know everything about me, Cy Bombay. You think you have me pegged, don't you?" Her anger was rising. At least, that was what the red color climbing her neck said. "It makes me so angry that you could be mad about Drew when you play your story so close to the vest!"

"What story? I don't have a story!" Okay, so I did. And it was a whopper. But that was beside the point. I'd been up-front with her about my life, my education and my history with women.

"Well, for one thing, why do you have a Dutch mercenary tied up in the bathroom of your private jet?"

"Did you forget that Dekker tried to kill you? That he tried to kill me?" I was getting pissed off now.

"I don't know why you couldn't have let the authorities in Mongolia have him after he kidnapped me. I don't understand why you couldn't deal with

Interpol or any other authorities. Why didn't you just turn him over to the airport security in London instead of dragging him along with us?"

She had me there. All those points made sense. There really was no way to tell her without explaining that killing Dekker was part of my job. That was something I knew I could never tell Veronica.

"Are you going to kill Arje, Cy?"

I had no answer for her.

Ronnie drew herself up to her full height. She'd made some kind of decision. "I will tell you the truth about Drew. I love him. That's all you need to know." She spun on her heel and went inside the house, slamming the door behind her.

It took everything I had to get back into the car and start the ignition. Unfortunately, I looked at the window and watched as Drew draped his arm around Veronica and kissed her forehead.

I made the twenty-minute trip back to Cedar Rapids in eight minutes. During that time, my brain was turned inside out. Why didn't she tell me about this Drew character? Clearly they had a relationship by the way he touched her. And that looked like a house, not an apartment I dropped her off at.

Oh, my God. She totally played me with that innocent bullshit! And I fell for it for the first time in fifteen years. She even pretended to love my guinea pig! Sartre was made a fool of! Well, I couldn't stand for that.

The pilot wisely said nothing as I climbed on the jet

and told him to take me to Santa Muerta to dispose of Arje Dekker.

I don't remember much of the flight. I had a major headache, and I don't get headaches. Ever. Somehow we crossed Central and South America and landed on the Bombay family's private island before I could string a sentence together.

Mum was standing on the airstrip, waiting for me. Apparently, the pilot had let them know I was coming, and she'd made the trip to meet me there.

I dragged Dekker off the plane and tossed him roughly onto the tarmac. Mum threw her arms around me, but I felt like I was made of stone.

"How was your trip, Squidgy?" she asked.

"It sucked." I pointed to Arje. "I have to kill this guy."

My mother looked from me to Dekker. She pulled out her cell and dialed.

"Carlos?" She spoke in perfectly accented Spanish, asking one of the staff members to come and get my vic and take him to the holding area. None of the staff on the island spoke English, and every last one of them was male. They never asked questions and got paid handsomely for their work. Carlos wouldn't have to kill the vic. That was a Bombay job. But he could take him to a room below the main level that was basically an escape-proof cell.

"Come on, dear," Mum said, taking my hand. "When was the last time you ate?"

I didn't really feel like eating. But I allowed her to

take me to the dining hall and set before me a plate of my favorite food. In case you are wondering, it was tomato soup and grilled cheese sandwiches. With all my worldly experience, that was what I wanted to come home to.

Mum watched me eat without saying a word. She knew something was up. She also knew that I wouldn't talk before I was ready. I felt like a stubborn child, but was in no way interested in a conversation about how Veronica Gale played me for an idiot.

So my mother chattered on about my cousins, Dad and the weather. I took in the information but it never registered.

"Why don't you let us take care of your vic?" Mum's words caught me up short. "You look like you could use a break."

I shook my head. "No. It's my job. I just need to get some sleep. I'll take care of him tomorrow."

She nodded, patted my hand and left. I finished up and, after liberating a bottle of twenty-five-year-old scotch from the bar, headed up to my room.

As I mentioned, the Bombay family has their own island. This is where the council stays most of the time and runs the actual family business. My cousin Missi and her sons live here year-round. The island is our home base. We have family reunions here every five years where we get to hang out, have our evaluations and sometimes take a turn on the ropes course.

Santa Muerta is virtually invisible to the rest of the

world. The main rule is that everyone goes inside between four p.m. and six p.m. to avoid notice from the various spy satellites overhead at that time. The island resembles a resort, with a main building where every Bombay has his or her own suite of rooms.

My room was just as I'd left it less than one year ago at the last reunion. Bookshelves covered the walls, full of well-worn books. The furniture was overstuffed leather—perfect for curling up and contemplating the mysteries of life.

I took a glass and two ice cubes with the bottle of scotch out onto the terrace. There was a great view of the ocean. The scotch was an Islay single-malt. It went down smooth to mend my frayed nerves. But it did little to ease my mind. How in the name of Immanuel Kant did I get mixed up with Veronica Gale? I thought I had her all figured out. Boy, was I wrong. The irony of this thought was not lost on me, but I was too upset to be rational. Was her whole "poor little orphan girl" thing some kind of con? If so, why me? And who the hell was Drew?

Thinking back to the first day I met her didn't help. All it did was give me goose bumps. I pictured her and remembered what she said. But there was no clue—nothing that made her seem other than how I'd pegged her.

My thoughts reeled back to Miami and how we met there. But no matter how many times I replayed the scenes, I found nothing that tipped me off. Mongolia swam into view, but the memories were too fresh. I felt nothing but pain and embarrassment when I remembered the month there with her.

My scotch went dry as I contemplated how I could have done things differently. The surf crashed against the rocks, and I sympathized. Those rocks were taking the same beating I did. Veronica had gotten under my skin in a way no woman had since Frannie Smith.

I poured another glass, wincing at the name of the first woman who'd played me for a fool. I guessed that all those years my subconscious controlled my desire for a relationship to protect me. And I blew it by falling for Ronnie.

Damn. Did I really just think that? I turned the idea over in my mind, searching for holes. But no, it was too late. I had fallen in love with her. And she made me look like an idiot. I pictured her even now sitting with the handsome Drew, laughing at how she'd played me. Would she tell him that she slept with me? Probably not. The woman was a liar. And I'd saved her life.

Then again, she'd been in danger in the first place only because of her connection to me. I couldn't really blame her for that. My thoughts turned to my prisoner three floors below. Chances were the staff had fed him. For a moment, I felt kind of friendly toward him. I had no idea why.

The sun set on my gloomy mood, and I nursed the bottle as the sky changed from turquoise to navy. No matter what I did, I still felt worse than stupid. And as I drank, my mood darkened.

Various thoughts popped into my head over the course of the evening. I thought of looking up Drew and killing him, but he wasn't the real culprit. Isn't it strange how your mind plays tricks on you? I imagined him making love to her and ended up hurling my bottle into the sea. That sucked, because I didn't like littering. Veronica Gale had made me look like an idiot, and she made me litter. I hated her for that.

Chapter Twenty-eight

Samuel: Your resume is quite impressive. Sixteen
years of military experience, extensive counter-
terrorism work. I'm surprised anyone could afford
you. What's the catch?
Creasy: I drink.

—*MAN ON FIRE*

"Are you going to kill me or what?" a tired and bored
Arje Dekker asked me an hour later. I sat across from
him in the holding room. He was chained to the wall
in a way that allowed him to move around a cot, chair
and toilet. I was perfectly safe. A little drunk, but
okay.

"I just don't get it," I droned on for the fortieth
time. "How did I miss it?"

Dekker rubbed his eyes. "I've told you, I don't know.
I thought she was this naive little schoolgirl too."

I sat up. "I never thought she was naive." I poured
Arje another paper cup half-full of scotch and with-
drew to a safe distance.

He drained it in one gulp. That made me sad inside. It was no way to treat such a good single-malt.

"Look, Bombay, what does it matter in the grand
scheme of things? We're men of action."

I giggled at his words and he smirked.

"Men like us don't get used by women. We use women."

"I don't use women, Dekker."

An ugly smile crossed his face. "Oh, no? Ronnie said you had all kinds of rich-housewife carney groupies. Are you telling me you weren't taking advantage of their fantasies to get laid?"

"You know," I said a little too slowly, "your English is really good for a Dutch mercenary."

"If you aren't going to take this seriously, then just leave so I can get some sleep before I'm killed."

I shook my head. "Extra sleep isn't going to help, my friend."

"And drinking yourself into a stupor over that little bitch isn't helping you either."

"Hey! Don't call her that!" I rose to my feet to . . . to do what? I sat back down.

We didn't speak for a moment. I did refill his cup. To his credit, he drank slower this time.

"I don't know why you are talking to me about this," Dekker said quietly. "I've got no experience with feelings toward a woman."

I lifted my glass to the light and turned it slowly, examining the amber fluid. "Well, I guess I just needed someone to talk to."

He snorted. "And you thought that someone was me? I am surprised. After all, you see me as some kind of genocidal monster."

I was a little defensive. "I've seen your file, Arje. I've

seen what you have done to women and children. Just for fun."

Dekker shook his head. "Back to that, are we?"

"Are you denying it?"

That would be stupid. I don't believe everything I read. But the Bombay network has always been completely accurate. Why would the council lie about Dekker's history?

"Yes. I am denying it."

"Well, that's damned convenient," I shouted. "Now that you face your death, I'm not surprised that you'd recant."

"How can I recant something I never said in the first place?" Arje said quietly. "You are the one with the faulty source, not me."

I started to pour more scotch, but stopped myself. "Let's drop it. I shouldn't have come down here." I stood and collected my bottle.

He looked me in the eyes, causing me to sit back down. "I guess if I was to have any regrets, that might be the big one." He rubbed the stubble on his chin. "It would've been nice to be in love. You got that over me."

I snorted. "Yeah. And I really picked a good one."

Arje Dekker got up from his chair, walked over to his cot and lay down on it. "Turn out the lights when you go. I need to get my beauty rest for the execution to come."

I didn't want to go. I wanted to talk more. But I did

as he asked and left him. I took the bottle of scotch with me. I'm not a total idiot.

Sartre's shrieks woke me from a dream where Dekker and I were in the Brazilian jungle fighting off a tribe of Amazonian women who all resembled Veronica Gale. Staggering from my bed, I pulled some fruit from the basket on the table and broke it up, tossing it inside her cage. While she jumped greedily on the mango, I had the distinct impression she was pissed off at me for my lack of presentation.

A knock at the door revealed my mother and father holding a platter of scrambled eggs, sausage and biscuits. I wearily let them in. After all, it had been a long time since I'd had eggs. There weren't many chickens in Mongolia.

"That's my boy." Dad smacked me on the back, launching my hangover into overdrive. I excused myself to clean up a bit. One shower later I was clean. Hungover, but clean.

"Your mum says you aren't yourself," Dad said with a grin. "She thinks it's because of some lady friend in Mongolia."

"I'm all right," I managed as I finished my second helping of eggs. The food was giving me a little strength. "It's nothing."

My parents looked at each other. They'd always been able to read me. I'd been lucky in that they never once questioned anything I did. They seemed just as proud of my decision to become a carney as they were when I got my Ph.D. from Yale. This prying into my emotional affairs was something new.

"Squidge," Mum started, "I'm a little worried about you."

"Why?" I'd given them no reason to worry. How did they know?

Mum handed half an orange to Sartre, who was our living centerpiece, before continuing. "You haven't killed your vic yet. That's not like you."

Oh. This was pretty unusual for a Bombay. There had been rare occasions when one of us would drag a live one home, or there wouldn't be holding cells on the property. But keeping one alive so I could get relationship advice from him must have seemed a bit strange.

"I saw the surveillance tapes and know you went in there, but we're having some difficulty with the sound." Mum frowned. "I don't know what we were thinking, sending Missi off on assignment. Nothing works here without her."

"You were spying on me?" I asked.

Dad nodded and my mother shot him a deadly look, causing him to dive into another helping of sausage.

"I was worried about you. Is there something you are trying to get out of him before you take him out?"

That sounded good. "Yes. He has some information I need and he's not coughing it up." She would believe that. Obviously a vic wasn't going to spill his guts before we literally spilled his guts. He'd try to keep any information he had to prolong his life span.

"Oh. Okay." Mum looked distracted. "So, when will you do it then?"

I sighed and leaned back from the table. "Soon. I promise. I just have to do a little research first. That's all."

We finished breakfast and, after kicking my parents out of my rooms, I hit my laptop. There were a couple of things I wanted to look up before I did anything else.

The next two days were a blur. I spent a lot of time online and calling in favors to get some information. My mother made frequent visits to see when I was going to clear my assignment. I didn't see the other members of the council, but I knew she was getting pressure on this.

The hardest part was forcing myself not to find out who Drew was. It wasn't easy, but I was so torn up about Veronica's admission that I just couldn't bring myself to do it. Drew seemed like a nice guy. Who was I to say otherwise? Besides, cyberstalking him would probably just make me mad. And I might find out he's a better man than me. That would suck big-time.

"So, what do you think?" I said to Dekker on one of my late-night visits to his cell. I made sure to permanently disable the sound on the surveillance cameras. It was just enough to confuse the council but not enough to incur Missi's wrath when she returned.

Dekker rubbed his face. "Jesus, Cy. Will you just

end it already? I swear that your drama is making me want to kill myself."

"Come on, just one more answer." He was right: This was beyond weird. I was the first to admit it. But something about these midnight sessions made me feel a little better. I thought that Dekker should be happy he was helping in some minor way. Apparently, he wasn't.

"Okay, okay. I think you should just confront her."

"What? You've been telling me all this time that I should forget about her! How can you flip-flop like that?"

"You obviously need closure." He held out his hand. "Now can I please have my cyanide pill?"

"You want to die now?" That was a shock.

"No. But this is beyond annoying. You are keeping me alive to be your analyst. And after all this time, you still haven't asked me about the truth."

I shook my head. "Not this again. Everyone on death row says they're innocent. And more than likely they're not. Why should I believe you?"

Dekker spread his hands wide. "I'm not going to beg. I've done some bad stuff in my career. But you keep accusing me of genocide and torture. And while I'm guilty of many things, those two are not on the list."

I cocked my head to the side, feeling a little like a spaniel who thought he might have heard the word *treat* but wasn't sure. "Look. My evidence is credible. And you admit you've committed acts of evil. Why should I believe you?" Seriously, this saw was getting dull.

"Why do you insist on pigeonholing me?" he said quietly, and the words shook me.

"What . . . what did you say?"

"You heard me, Bombay." Dekker steepled his fingers. "I have killed a lot of men. Most of them were armed. I've given orders for torture to retrieve information. But I've never directly participated in it, nor have I ordered the torture of civilians. I've been paid handsomely for my work. But I've never tolerated the torture or murder of women or children." He punctuated his monologue with a shrug.

I stared at Arje Dekker for a long time. His words wormed their way through my brain and froze there. They caused just enough doubt . . . just enough to make me stop and think. Oh, there was no doubt when it came to the fact that Dekker was a gun for hire. There was no doubt that he'd chosen to work for whoever paid him most, good or bad. But the fact that some of what he said made me question my beliefs was important. Dekker might, indeed, be innocent of the gravest offenses—the ones that would make me want to kill him.

"You're right," I said finally. "I did pigeonhole you." His expression did not change as I continued. "And maybe that makes you right about other things too." I stood, gave him a brief nod, and left Arje Dekker alive.

Chapter Twenty-nine

Dignon: Just hear me out. It's called Hinckley Cold Storage. Here are just a few of the key ingredients; dynamite, pole-vaulting, laughing gas, choppers—can you see how incredible this is gonna be? Hang gliding, come on!

—*BOTTLE ROCKET*

I knocked on the door and stepped back to await an answer. Nothing. I rapped a little more firmly. Still nothing. It was two o'clock on a sunny afternoon. I decided to wait it out on the swing on the porch.

A few neighbors gave me odd glances as they came and went, but no one said anything. It was a hot day, but I sat in the shade and there was a slight breeze. My quarry would be home soon enough. And then I would have the answers I needed to send me back to my RV. I might even be able to hook up with a few county fairs before state fair season. The thought of that made me smile.

"Cy?" Ronnie seemed shocked as she came up the sidewalk. She looked around furtively. "What are you doing here?"

I rose from my seat and said nothing as she approached. I didn't owe her anything more than what I had in my hands. I'd fulfilled my promise. That was all that was important.

What I'd underestimated was the effect seeing her again would have on me. My stomach shrank and my heart skipped several beats, no matter how calm I tried to appear. I hoped she wouldn't notice.

The sun illuminated her light blonde hair. The pale skin that had made me shiver in Mongolia had been replaced by a bronzed glow. It took everything I had not to scoop her up and carry her up to her bed. Until I remembered that it wasn't just her bed, but Drew's as well. The lust was instantly replaced with anger. Anger was good. I could handle anger.

"Don't worry," I said as nonchalantly as I could (which was considerably less nonchalantly than I'd hoped). "I just had to drop something off."

She looked around. "Did you talk to Drew?"

"Again, don't worry. I have nothing to tell him. What happened in Mongolia stays in Mongolia." She started to speak, but I didn't want to hear it. "Besides, I'm just fulfilling my promise to you." I handed her the envelope I had brought with me and turned and walked away.

"You are an arrogant idiot," she shouted after me, but I didn't give her the satisfaction of turning around. Mostly because she was right about the idiot part. I didn't need anyone to remind me of that.

"Quit running away from your problems and talk to me, dammit!" Ronnie shouted.

I turned and stormed back to her. "You are not my

problem. I am my problem. The fact that I fell in love with you on the steppes of Mongolia is my problem. But you don't love me. You told me that last time I was here."

"I never said I didn't love you," she said quietly.

"You said you loved Drew. That was enough." I left out the other complications, mainly that she would never fit into my world and her mere existence would constantly remind me of my faults. I could never tell her that.

"Why do you want to walk away?" she asked.

"I don't want to. I don't like walking away. I just feel that this is what is best for both of us." *What is best for me.* "I want you, and I can't have you."

"What . . . what does that mean?" Ronnie's voice quavered, cutting me to the quick.

"Trust me, Ronnie. Pigeonholing me is just the tip of the iceberg. You don't want to know about what's beneath the water." Ooh. That was good. A *Titanic* reference. Was that the best I could do?

"You are saying I don't want to know who you really are?"

I shook my head. "I'm saying I don't want you to know who I really am." With that, I turned and headed for the car.

Good-bye, Veronica Gale. And that would be the last time I would ever let my heart get in the way of my dignity.

I was mildly surprised as I drove away that she didn't run after me. What did I expect? That she'd throw herself at my feet and beg my forgiveness? That clearly wasn't going to happen. I must admit I did check the rearview mirror. She looked pissed. Her arms were folded over her chest and her face was red. That was a little bit satisfying.

Within twenty-four hours, I was back in my motor home, driving aimlessly around the state of Ohio. Why? I don't know. It just seemed like a good idea at the time. Sartre had mellowed somewhat after her international adventures. I took in a movie now and then and had dinner wherever I stopped for the night. I was getting my groove back by burying the memories of betrayal.

Ronnie didn't e-mail me. Not that I expected her to after what I'd dropped off. I'm sure she was not happy to find a complete file on the wrongdoings of one Senator William Anderson. Oh, yes, the sexual liaisons were just a small part of what that man had done wrong. I gave her a two-inch-thick file folder detailing some pretty shady money-laundering schemes involving the French government and several accounts of bribery in a "pay to play" scam he was running. I was pretty sure she hated me now.

I didn't feel the need to give her too much information. I wanted an *I told you so* moment but didn't want to crush her completely. Oh, and I also looked up Drew. It wasn't hard to find out who he was. Not that I would do anything with the information.

Turned out Drew was Drew Connery, a Rhodes

scholar and former campaign manager for the Johnson County Democrats. He ran a Web site on the conspiracy theories behind Senator Anderson's death. Well, great. I hope she shared the information I gave her with him. Let them both stew in their sullenness.

Okay, so I entertained a few fantasies of smashing his face in, strapping him to a space shuttle or feeding him to a pool full of piranha. But I thought there was something to be said for not acting on that.

I went back to Santa Muerta to make sure Dekker was all right. Without consulting anyone, I took him with me off the island. It was a pretty drastic act on my part. But until I could sort things out, I wasn't quite ready to kill him. And if I didn't, the council would.

"Why am I here?" Dekker asked as he sat in my favorite chair drinking my favorite scotch.

"Because I don't want to kill you," I said as I chopped up a salad for Sartre.

"And why don't you want to kill me?"

"I've changed my mind."

Dekker chuckled at that. No doubt he found this whole scenario amusing. I'd rigged up an ankle-and-wrist collar system loosely based on the invisible fencing idea for dogs. If he tried to lunge, kick or leave, he'd be shocked senseless.

"Nice place you got here," he continued. "Like a mobile command base."

I nodded. "You should see my summer home. It's a Volkswagen Microbus."

I Shot You Babe

My guest laughed at that. That was odd—thinking of him as my guest instead of my vic. It was only a matter of time before the council caught on to the fact that I hadn't cleared my assignment.

Interestingly enough, just as I thought this, my cell phone rang.

"This is Coney," I answered, hoping it was just my dad calling with the football scores. I didn't really follow the game, but he didn't need to know that.

"Coney? It's your aunt Carolina. Where is Dekker?"

"What? You mean he's missing?"

"I've sent you something." She hung up before I could respond. Within seconds, a UPS courier knocked on my door.

"Dude, you are hard to find," the pimply kid said as I signed the release for the package.

"Apparently not," I replied as I shut the door in his face. Sartre mistook the sound for the fridge door and began *wheek*ing. I tossed her some spinach and sat down to open the envelope I'd been sent.

Son of a bitch.

If I were to look at things philosophically, I would have to say that I am not a paranoid person. I knew the council watched us to an extent, but I didn't think they knew everything about us. At least, I didn't before I opened that damned envelope.

There were a lot of things going through my mind as I drove through the night to Iowa. I injected Dekker with a sleeping agent. He let me. Maybe he was tired

231

of all this too. Once the caffeine kicked into over-drive, even stranger thoughts took over. I toyed with the idea of the existence of God. Something larger than me seemed to be at work here. That was the only way to explain how I got a summons from the council asking me to return to Santa Muerta with both Dekker and one Veronica Gale.

Oh, sure, it might have been a coincidence. I'd feel a whole lot better if that were the case. It would be so convenient to believe that. But this all seemed too ar-ranged. After five hours of trying to figure out how it happened, I gave up and pulled into a Wal-Mart park-ing lot in the Quad Cities to get some sleep.

I reread the file. There was no doubting its intent. I was being ordered to bring these two people before the council. They had a lot of questions. And it was my guess that they wouldn't let either Ronnie or Arje live through the day. That wasn't like the council. Well, it was exactly like the old council. But our folks were in charge now, and they were different. At least, they were supposed to be.

I probably don't need to mention that I didn't sleep well. I thought about leaving Dekker there and just going myself to the island. I sure as hell didn't want to involve Ronnie in any of this. But if I left them here, it could be a trap, and someone else from the family might grab them or worse. What a mess. Freud didn't have dilemmas like this.

As I downed my coffee the next morning, I realized something: I was in Carolina Bombay's hometown. I could stop by and see her and ask her about my orders. Yes. That would work. Aunt Carolina would have to give me something to work with. Mainly because I wouldn't leave her house until she did.

I called first, because I'm not rude. Carolina sounded thrilled that I was in town. By the time I got to her house, my cousins Gin and Dak had joined her for a little family reunion. In spite of the fact that this was business, I was happy to see them.

"Coney!" Gin squealed as she hugged me. Dak grinned from behind her, holding his son's hand. Louis smiled up at me.

"Hey, cuz. Great to see you two." And I meant it.

Carolina emerged from the dining room carrying a tiny, redheaded infant. She introduced the baby as Dak and Leonie's daughter, Sofia.

"You guys sure are settling down," I observed. Never in my wildest dreams would I have imagined Dak married with kids.

"So when will this happen to you?" Gin asked.

I winced. A month or so ago, I would've thought it possible. Now it seemed like I would never start a family. With a twinge of surprise, I found myself feeling sad about that.

I took the baby from my aunt and cradled her in my arms. "I don't think so." Sofia cooed and promptly fell asleep. She smelled like talcum powder, and I realized I was sniffing her head.

"Yeah, right." Dak laughed.

I tried to smile. I really did. But something about

holding that baby made me feel sick inside. I cursed the Bombay family for taking this chance away from me. Carolina brought out some wine and cheese, then took the baby back. I watched her expression of un-adulterated bliss.

"I know Georgia would be a wonderful grand-mother," Carolina said, looking directly at me.

"I think you're right," I said. But that was impossible. First of all, my idiot brother, Richie, had to go and get himself killed—which was okay, because I was pretty sure any spawn he had would've been born with the mark 666. And second, well, unless I got a surrogate, there wasn't much hope for my procreating.

"What brings you to the area?" Gin asked as her daughter, Romi, burst into the room only long enough to grab her cousin Louis and run off.

"An assignment. Your mom called. I thought I'd get some details."

I watched as everyone looked at one another. While it wasn't unheard-of for Bombays to talk over their assignments, it was still pretty rare.

"Should we leave?" Dak started to rise to his feet.

I waved him back down. "No. Stay. It doesn't mat-ter to me."

In fact, the only person it would matter to was Carolina. She was a member of the council. If it was top-secret, she'd let us know.

My aunt seemed to think about this for a moment. "No, it's okay. What did you want to know?"

"Why do you want me to bring these two people back to Santa Muerta?"

"What two people?" Gin asked.

"My girlfriend and my former vic." There was a stunned hush. I don't know if that was because they were surprised I had a girlfriend or at the fact that any vic was considered "former" and not "late."

Carolina nodded. "You didn't clear your assignment. You brought Vic to the island, then took him off . . . alive. We want to know why."

"And the reason I am supposed to bring Veronica Gale into all of this?"

"We think she knows too much," Carolina said slowly. She knew she had to be careful. Both Gin and Dak had involved their mates in the family and almost had to kill them.

"I was careful," I said, hoping that would be enough.

"We have to make sure," my aunt said evenly. "For everyone's safety."

"I can't let you kill her. I won't allow it. If we leave her alone, she will never know anything."

Carolina shook her head. "You know the rules, Coney. Unless you marry her and tell her everything, she is dangerous to the family."

"That's not going to happen, Aunt Carolina." I felt a stab of pain. I wanted to marry Ronnie. But there were too many complications.

"What?" Gin shouted. "That's so wrong!"

"What are you complaining about?" Dak asked her. "You're retired, remember?"

His sister shot him a look that would've eaten paint off a wall.

"That doesn't matter. I still think it's unfair."

Carolina spoke up. "This is the wrong business for fairness, Gin."

"I don't like it either," Dak said. I was thinking I might not have to say anything at all. "The council once put a hit on my wife."

His mother nodded. "I can see that. However, sometimes there are gray areas when it comes to a job. It's not easy to come up with reasons all the time. You will just have to trust that the council knows what it's doing."

That stopped us all short. Trust wasn't exactly a typical family trait with the Bombays. In fact, it was usually quite the opposite.

"Well, I think that's bullshit," Gin spit.

Carolina snapped, "You will not swear around Sofia!" She even covered the sleeping infant's ears.

"It is bullshit, Mom." Dak's temper was rising. "I think there should be a family meeting about this."

"We've never had a family meeting to decide how the council does things. Not in four thousand years," Carolina said calmly. "The business is evolving."

"And what if we refuse?" Gin asked. Clearly she forgot that she was the only Bombay ever given retirement. But I admired the fact that she was sticking up for the rest of us.

"Don't tell me how to do my job," Carolina snapped.

Dak stood up and pointed at his mother. "This is wrong. And you know it."

"What do you think, Coney?" Gin asked.

"I think I'm tired of this whole mess."

Dak frowned. "What do you mean?"

I stood up. "I'm sick of the fact that we can't get involved with people without the scrutiny of the council, wanting to know everything."

"And what about your vic, Coney?" Carolina asked calmly. "Why didn't you clear your assignment?"

It was a good question. A fair one. "I just didn't feel like it."

Gin and Dak looked from me to their mother, who stared openmouthed at me.

"Coney, you know the rules," Carolina said steadily. "We have a client who paid us to have Vic killed. You don't get to say no."

I shrugged. "Well, this time I did." I understood this was earth-shattering. Dekker wasn't a saint. He was a bad guy. But there was more to it than that. And maybe after four thousand years, it was time to say, *Enough*.

"Do not put us in this position," Carolina pleaded. "I don't want to sign your death warrant. I don't want to do that to your mother. She's already lost Richie."

"Do what you must," I said, wondering if she would kill me right then and there.

"Mom?" Gin said weakly as her brother sat down and dropped his face into his hands. "Mom, you can't take Coney out. He must have a good reason for not killing his vic."

"You aren't going to do that, right?" Gin repeated. I knew what was going through her mind. It was the same thing Dak and I were thinking. This would either be the end of the Bombay family business or the end of me. The shock crackled in the atmosphere that hung around us like lead weights.

Romi shouted from the yard, and Louis came running in. "Grandma! Romi got a splinter in her elbow!" He tugged on his grandmother's sleeve, and she passed the baby to Dak and left.

"Coney, are you really going to stand up to the council?" Gin asked.

"Yes. I'm done."

Dak spoke up. "You know, our generation of the family has really been through the shit. And I'm willing to go to bat for you, Coney."

"I thought we'd gotten rid of the bad council," said Gin, referring to a coup that had forced our grandparents into early retirement.

"Why would Mom behave just like her mother?" Dak said.

My mum was on the council too. Which meant that she knew about this assignment and hadn't told me. Another wave of shock engulfed me. How could this have happened? And what in the hell were we going to do about it?

Chapter Thirty

Dubanich: "Do you know anything about airplane design?"
Nate: "Yeah, I could give it a shot. You know, you get me a pencil and one of those little rulers."

—*LEVERAGE*

Dak, Gin and I wasted no time. We dropped the kids off with Diego and Leonie and locked Dekker in Gin's basement. Afterward we picked up our other cousins Liv and Paris and strategically retreated to my latest Wal-Mart parking lot home. We needed to talk through this newest family development. But in true Bombay form, none of us felt safe discussing it where we might be overheard.

"I'm so sick of this family," Liv said as she held Sartre in her arms.

"What are we going to do about it?" asked Paris. It was a good question. Something had to be done. The five of us agreed we didn't want to blindly answer to the council anymore.

"Thank God you got this assignment." Gin flipped through the file. "I would've taken him out without talking to him."

Dak nodded. "All my files have had a laundry list of bad deeds that would make Saddam Hussein blush."

"So why now?" Paris asked. We all turned to stare at him. "Why didn't we fight this a long time ago?"

I ran my fingers through my hair. "I don't know if you guys should be involved. This is my problem."

"It's time. I think I speak for all of us when I say we want retirement," Liv said.

"I'm tired of the fact that it's taken for granted that you can't trust anyone in the Bombay family," Dak replied. He looked tired. Shock would do that to you.

"I've always trusted you guys," Gin said slowly.

"I don't want to be responsible for killing off an entire generation of Bombays," I said. "I'll do it alone."

Paris jumped to his feet and started pacing—no easy feat considering there were five people crowded into my RV. "Well, we have to do something. I'm tired of it too."

Liv reached out and patted her brother on the arm. There was something about that gesture that soothed me. And I realized that Gin was right: I'd always trusted my cousins—the Bombays of my generation. This was a new thing in the family. As far as I knew, that kind of camaraderie had always been discouraged before.

"I'm not going to kill Dekker," I declared. "In fact, I'm not going to kill anyone anymore."

My cousins turned to stare at me. Was the solution really this simple?

"Okay . . ." Paris spoke up. He was always the most practical and cautious of us. "But how are we going to do that without getting us all killed?"

"Good question," I said. "We will have to work together." That sounded good. How would we do it?

"Coney?" Gin asked. "What made you question this particular hit?"

Dak looked at her in that brotherly way that implied she was nuts. "I'd like to think that any one of us would have eventually done that."

She shook her head. "Not necessarily. I mean, with all the training that's been forced on us throughout our lives, it's been ingrained in us not to question anything."

We all thought about this for a moment. No one wanted to admit it, but she had a point.

"Something about this hit stood out," Gin persisted in a way that made me itch metaphorically. "What was it?"

I knew the answer. I wished I didn't, but I did. Veronica made me question the hit. And while I would have liked to believe I was smart enough to think critically regarding assignments, the truth was, we were trained to avoid dealing with the truth when it was inconvenient. Bombays were so brainwashed we might let something like this go by once—hell, maybe even twice—before asking about it.

"I've gotten involved with someone who made me realize you can't judge someone by their file," I said slowly, unsure how much I should reveal.

My cousins prompted me silently with their stares. There was no easy way out of this. So I spilled my guts. I told them everything. About how this woman made me question everything around me. And how Dekker had become my father confessor. And most of all, how I was just sick and tired of the violence and death that surrounded us.

I went into more detail about Ronnie. There was something very intimate about relating the story of my relationship to my cousins. I guess I'd gone it alone so long I didn't think I'd ever need someone to talk to. Gin, Dak, Liv and Paris listened patiently as I started with meeting Veronica in Nebraska to our angst-filled meeting when I dropped off the envelope containing Senator Anderson's sins. I guess I gave them a welcome distraction from our immediate problem. Once I finished, Gin pulled out her cell phone and ordered pizza while Dak ran across the parking lot to score a case of beer.

"Wow," Liv said softly. The look in her eyes told me she was impressed.

"And you didn't want to kill him?" Dak asked. Gin punched him in the arm. "Not even a little bit?"

I laughed and took a swig of beer. "Yeah, okay. Maybe I did a little bit."

Paris stared into space, chewing thoughtfully. "There were rumors of murder after Anderson's death." He shrugged. "I knew he was a prick so I never thought anything about it."

"Well, you can't serve Veronica up to the council," Dak said. "That's a bit of a deal breaker."

Gin punched him again. "And what about this Drew thing? Why didn't you give Veronica a chance to explain? Maybe once she found you, she didn't want him anymore."

Liv nodded. "You should have told her how you felt, Coney. Maybe that would've changed things."

Paris leaped to my defense. Good man. "She totally played him! This Ronnie never told Coney she was already in a relationship."

"Love is a little more complicated than that, little brother," Liv said. "You should never assume anything."

Gin nodded. "Coney can't do this by himself. And we can't let things keep going as they are."

"But you're retired!" Dak cried out again. "This doesn't even affect you!"

Gin shook her head. "As far as you guys are concerned, it does affect me."

"Okay," Liv said. "So let's do it."

Chapter Thirty-one

John Smith (at anniversary dinner in fine restaurant): So what do we do, Jane? Shoot it out here? Hope for the best?

Jane Smith: Well, that would be bad because they would probably ask me to leave once you are dead.

—*Mr. & Mrs. Smith*

"I'm not sure this is a good idea," I said to Sartre as I drove the remaining sixty miles to Iowa City. The guinea pig looked up at me from the passenger seat as if to say she didn't think she should be riding without a seat belt.

My cousins and I had agreed on this course of action the night before, but we'd had a lot of beer and may not have been thinking clearly. What we were about to do flew in the face of the Bombay family creed. We were confident that Missi would be on board with it, but there were five other cousins we hadn't consulted. Were we making a mistake?

Sartre *wheek*ed, implying that I was driving too fast. Maybe I should have put her back in her cage.

The thought of seeing Ronnie again twisted my intestines in a way I did not find very comfortable.

Seeing Drew again was a necessary evil. Seeing them together would probably burn out my eyes. But if I left them here and went off to confront the council, they might just get picked up anyway. The safest place for Ronnie was with me. Unfortunately, the council could use Drew to get to her. As much as I didn't want to admit it, both had to come with me.

I pulled off of I-80 and coasted into the very edge of the city. Stopping at the first car rental agency I found, I traded my RV for a black Kia minivan. What? Obviously I'm beyond the whole image thing or I wouldn't be driving a motor home, in the first place, and I'd have a rottweiler instead of a guinea pig in the second.

It only took fifteen minutes before I pulled up in front of Ronnie's house. This would have to be done very carefully. Carolina would have had time to alert the rest of the council to do . . . what? I had no idea, but I knew better than to underestimate them. Many a Bombay has been quite surprised to find their mother bursting through the door to gun them down. It has been known to happen.

This plan had me torn up inside. I wanted to help Ronnie because . . . well, because I loved her. I also did not want to help Ronnie, because she loved someone else. Oh, the philosophical questions.

Looking both ways, I raced up to the house and knocked on the door.

Veronica answered. "Cy? What the hell is going on?"

I pushed past her into the house. "Where's Drew? We've got to get going." I worked my way through the rooms while she followed.

"Stop! You can't just barge in here and make demands like that!" She grabbed me by the shoulder but I shrugged her off. "Cy! Dammit! Listen to me!"

I spun around to face her. "Ronnie. You and Drew are in danger. I need to get you out of here right now."

She folded her arms over her chest in a move I'd seen so many times before. "Don't be ridiculous. Why would Drew and I be in danger?"

"You met the kind of people I deal with back in Ulaanbaatar. I'd consider trusting me if I were you." *Yes. Trust me. Not like I can trust you, Ronnie. But you should trust me.*

She went pale, and I could see the name *Arje Dekker* on her lips. For a moment I thought I saw an unasked question in her eyes. She wondered what I had done with him. Something stopped her from asking.

"Drew?" she called. "Drew! We have to run an errand!"

Drew came down the stairs wearing nothing but a pair of jeans and deck shoes. His physique was flawless. The boyish way he smiled at me made me feel sick. I said nothing as he pulled on a T-shirt and followed us out to the van.

"Sartre!" Ronnie squealed as she scooped up the pig and buried her face in its fur. Sartre purred with glee. I drove the car as the woman I loved showed the man she loved *my* guinea pig.

"Where are we going?" Drew finally asked. He must have been incredibly trusting. Why on earth would he get into a car with a man he didn't know without asking before we left the house?

"Yes, Cy." Ronnie narrowed her eyes at me. "Where are we going?"

I could see Drew frowning in the rearview mirror.

"You mean you don't know?" he asked her.

Veronica looked at him, then me. She chewed her lip. In spite of myself I thought that was pretty damn adorable.

"Ronnie?" Drew asked. What kind of moron was he? You don't get into a vehicle with someone you don't know to go to an unknown location!

Veronica decided to answer him. "Remember when I told you about that guy who jumped me in Mongolia?"

"Is he after you?" Drew asked with surprise. Of course he'd be shocked. This was a man of education. In his world, men didn't beat one another up. They used words. And I used to be one of those bozos.

"No," I answered. "It's someone else." I glanced at Ronnie to check her reaction. Fear played across her features. She must have thought I'd killed Dekker eventually. Of course, she couldn't possibly know that I'd kept him alive for relationship advice and then refused to kill him.

"Then where are we going?" Drew was starting to grow a pair now. I wanted to hate him. I really did. But this wasn't his fault.

"Someone else is after you. We are going to the airport to board a private plane there."

Veronica and Drew simultaneously shouted, "Who?"

I said nothing, because there was nothing more to say.

Ronnie grew angry. "Who is after us?"

"No one is after you . . . yet," I said finally.

"But you said—" she started.

"I said nothing specific."

She looked at me, then glanced back at Drew, who now leveled his gaze on me. Well, really on the back of my head.

"It's just safer if you come with me," I said through gritted teeth.

"What? Why? Who would threaten our safety?"

We pulled up at the airport. It only took a moment to clear security and make our way to the hangar where the Bombay jet waited for us. As we boarded, I introduced Veronica and Drew to Gin, Dak, Liv and Paris.

My cousins started talking to Drew as I made my way toward the back of the plane.

"That's it, Cy!" Ronnie whispered urgently. "You are going to tell me what's going on, and you are going to tell me now!"

I turned to face her. "Did you tell Drew about me? Did you tell him what happened in Mongolia?"

She looked taken aback. "What are you talking about? And why is this all about you? You're the one who showed up demanding we go with you! Tell me right now who is after Drew and why!"

The look in her eyes stopped me short. She still had control over my emotions. And as much as I fought it, there was no denying that I was in love with her. "Apparently, I am the one who is a danger to you."

Chapter Thirty-two

Marv: I check the list. Rubber tubing, gas, saw, gloves, cuffs, razor wire, hatchet, Gladys, and my mitts.

—*SIN CITY*

"What . . . what did you say?" Veronica was shaken now. Her lip trembled, and immediately I wanted to take all the things I'd said back.

"Look." I ran my fingers through my hair. "Just go and sit down. I have a few phone calls to make."

"Cy! I want to—" she started, but I didn't let her finish.

"Dammit, Ronnie! Just go up front! I'll join you after I take care of something!" I'd never shouted at her before. I really rarely shouted at anyone. It wasn't my way. Anger wasn't my thing. So how did this woman inspire so much of it in me?

I didn't wait to see if she left before ducking into the back room. Using Missi's cell phone, I called the one person who could help us once we landed.

When I joined the group, there was enough tension in the air to choke a goat. A large goat with an enormous trachea. Ronnie sat alone in one of the seats, staring sullenly out the window. Drew was making banal conversation with Paris . . . something about research methods. Gin and Liv were looking at me meaningfully. Dak inclined his head toward Ronnie.

"I'm sorry," I said as I took the seat next to her. Ronnie glared at me before turning her attention back to the window.

"I shouldn't have come to your house and frightened you like that."

"Did you kill Dekker?" She asked the one question I wasn't expecting.

"No." I wasn't lying about that. Granted, I could've told her he was still alive, but I thought the less she knew, the better.

She turned her attention back to the window. I said nothing. Minutes passed. An hour passed. I was glad she didn't speak. Mainly because I didn't want to answer.

"How dare you?" she growled finally once we were flying over Mexico.

"Oh. You are talking to me."

"You are so arrogant! Where do you get off treating people like that?"

"Well, I—"

"You think you have it all figured out, don't you?" She was just warming up. "What makes you think you know me so well?"

"Clearly I didn't know you at all," I said softly.

She turned to face me. "And what in the hell do you mean by that?"

"You lied to me. You played me for a fool. And I fell

in love with you," I said simply, because there was no other way to say it.

Her face softened. "You . . . you fell in love with me?"

"Well," I said, "don't let it go to your head. Now that I know what you really are."

And then her face hardened. The angles were so sharp and fierce you could open a bottle on them. "And what am I really?"

"A con artist."

"What?" I was pretty sure her shriek could be heard on the ground.

"Like I said earlier: You played me. And you did such a good job I fell for it. Way to go."

"How did I play you? What are you talking about?"

I was getting tired of this wordplay. My head hurt, and I was concerned that my upcoming actions would have irrevocable consequences. Arguing with Ronnie would only dull my wits, and I needed them.

"You led me to believe you were single . . . unattached. You led me to believe you were innocent and naive. Hell, you even told me you lived in an apartment when you really had a huge house!"

Veronica opened her mouth. Then she closed it. She opened it again, but something stopped the words from coming out. Clearly she needed time to construct an argument now that she was busted. I got up and moved to sit with my cousins. We had some work to do.

"I can't believe we are doing this!" Liv whispered. "It's so exciting!"

Gin smiled and patted her best friend's hand. "Just remember to stick to the plan. If we all agree then there's nothing they can do."

Dak spoke up: "I love you."

His sister turned to him. "What?"

Dak continued. "It's true. You don't even need to be here. And yet you are. Way to go, sis."

Paris leaned in. "Are you sure we should land on the island? Maybe we should land in Ecuador and get a speedboat or something."

I shook my head. "No good. We have to make a statement. You all called your parents, right?"

Liv nodded. "I read Dad the riot act first. I want him to know what he's up against."

"We are taking a huge risk here," Paris replied.

I looked at my watch. "Let's hope we're right. Let's hope this works."

As if in answer to my words, the plane dropped in altitude. Within minutes we'd be arriving on the tarmac at Santa Muerta. And while I was hoping we'd survive the day, there was no way of knowing for sure.

"Cy." Veronica laid her hand on my arm as I prepared to exit the plane. "I need to talk to you."

"Not now, Ronnie." And I meant it. I needed to keep my focus sharp.

"Okay. But at least let me thank you."

This brought me up short, and I stopped in my tracks. "For what?"

"You are thinking of our best interests." She looked back at Drew. "You didn't have to do that."

"Believe me, Ronnie, what I am about to do will help me as much as it helps you." Provided we didn't die horrible deaths at the hands of our parents, that was.

"When you get back, I really need to talk to you."

I really didn't want to hear it. *Sorry, Cy. But I love him.* Even if it wasn't that, it would be something equally as hurtful. Maybe dying at the hands of my mother would be less painful.

"Fine," I answered, even though I didn't mean it. "We'll talk when I get back."

I had given Ronnie and Drew strict instructions not to leave the plane. It was for their own good. Granted, the council had no idea they were here, and why would they? It was the safest place for them to hide—right out in the middle of the battlefield.

The five of us Bombays made our way to the headquarters, where a weird family showdown was about to take place. A sort of bloodless intervention, so to speak. Only this would lead to our not killing anymore instead of not drinking or doing drugs. It was kind of poetic, once you thought about it.

We found the council in the conference room, waiting for us. Mum was there with her brother, York. On her left were her cousins, Carolina and Pete. To their right were her other cousins, Cali, Missi's mom, and her brother, Montgomery. For some reason the European branch was not represented, as their cousins Burma and Asia were missing. I didn't mind having fewer dangerous council members to deal with.

The Europeans were pretty laid-back. If we could make this happen, they would go along with it.

"Sit down, kids." Mum motioned to the opposite side of the table. We took our seats. This was going to be a little awkward.

"It has come to our attention," Uncle York began, "that you don't approve of our policies." He said it as though we were naughty employees in the boardroom. Hell, he was even wearing a suit.

This was unexpected politeness. With many families there was at least shouting and expletives . . . maybe a hurled beer bottle. In our family at this point the pistols usually came out. Mexican standoffs were de rigueur. We were trained at the age of eight in how to deal with that situation.

"That's right," Gin said loudly.

Carolina shook her head. "Gin, you shouldn't even be here. You're retired."

Gin slammed her hand down on the table. "Why does everyone keep saying that? I'm really getting pissed off about that!"

"She really is," Dak said in a stage whisper to his mother. "You should've heard her on the plane."

Carolina turned to me. "Coney, are you refusing to accept your assignment?"

I nodded. "That's right."

Mum clapped her hands together. "You have to kill Dekker. You have to bring Veronica Gale here."

I shook my head. "No."

My mother looked from her left to her right. "We

have a contract to honor. And we need to know more about Gale and her friend." She looked at the folder in front of her. "This Drew Connery could be a terrorist."

"No. Being a Rhodes scholar does not qualify him as a terrorist. The Republicans tried that with Clinton and it didn't stick. Both Veronica and Drew are innocent of what happens here."

Uncle York spoke up. "Look, I don't care about the other two, but we have a contract for Dekker's head. We can't ignore that."

Cali agreed. "The Bombays have given out assignments to be accepted without question for four millennia. Why should you get to question things?"

"Why not?" came a voice over the PA. Cali cringed as the voice of her daughter bellowed from the speakers overhead. "For chrissake, Mom! You sent me on a damned reality show, where I almost killed the wrong guy, just so you could set me up with a man!" Missi appeared in the doorway and walked toward us. There she was, my ace in the hole. And I knew her recent experience gave the council reason to rethink this.

"And you did find a man!" Cali seemed surprised her daughter wouldn't get the logic. "You found Lex! Because of us!"

Missi stopped and placed her hands on her hips. "This is idiotic. You are all manipulating us into doing whatever you want! You're using these assignments to run our lives!"

Our parents looked at one another. Did they get it?

"The truth is," I said, "we aren't going to work for the family business anymore." I gave them a moment to let it sink in. By the looks on their faces, I was pretty sure they hadn't seen that coming.

"And we are conducting an audit to review our finances," Paris added.

"And we never, ever want to know if we have killed anyone who didn't deserve it." Liv's voice trembled with rage.

The council was stunned. They had no idea we would demand the disbanding of the family industry. In the past, the old guard would have shot us. Would they do that?

"You can't just quit!" York protested. Somehow I took his words to mean that we couldn't quit because he was never able to.

Paris sputtered, "This isn't a fraternity! You can't just do things because they were done to you."

"Don't you see?" Dak said calmly. "The time for things like this is over. The Dark Ages ended centuries ago. This is civilization. We can't keep killing people."

Liv shouted, "And we sure as hell aren't going to kill anyone just because you think we should!"

"We won't allow it," Cali said with steel in her voice.

There it was. The threat.

"Are you going to kill your own children?" Gin shouted. "We represent the majority of our generation. You'll be wiping us out."

"And you'll have to raise our kids!" Dak threw in somewhat unhelpfully. From what I'd heard about Carolina Bombay's obsession with babies, I thought that was more of a strike against us.

Missi joined us at the table but didn't sit down. "You will have to kill us. Because we are never going to kill anyone for you again."

I fist-bumped her. It wasn't something I'd ever done, and likely wasn't something I'd ever do again, but I did it anyway.

Chapter Thirty-three

Agent Sands (in Marlon Brandon voice): Failure to appear at meetings at designated times will result in forfeiture of protection . . . protection you will definitely need.

—*ONCE UPON A TIME IN MEXICO*

If you are going to make an ultimatum, you have to be ready to back it up. Once you say with absolute certainty that you will not do something, there is no going back. The Bombays have followed this flawed logic with a religious zeal that would have made Hitler envious. Family members who refused to participate in the business were "liquidated" immediately—usually by another family member.

It was a delicate and unstable way to approach life, but that was our culture. Some cultures wrestled over their differences. Others used a game of chess or a "dance-off." We usually made one another bleed to death. Every family was different.

I was not an only child. But my brother had been such a supreme asshole that I felt like one. Dak and Paris had their sisters. They were lucky. And I was lucky that they included me in that group. And it helped make it that much harder for the council to disagree with us if they had to wipe out all their children. That was a plus for us.

So we glared at one another over a conference table for at least ten minutes, each side hoping the other would suddenly jump up and laugh and yell, "Just kidding!" But that wasn't going to happen. And we'd use shrapnel instead of confetti.

We'd made a very dangerous move here. And we weren't even armed. Well, Missi was. She had a button that could electrocute the council. Hopefully we wouldn't need to use it.

While we sat there in silence, each side hoping their glares were dramatic enough to influence the others, all I could think of was Ronnie. I had it bad. It sucked that she loved Drew. But even if I died, she'd live—I'd tipped the pilot a lot to take them back home if we didn't return. I hoped she'd take care of Sartre. I loved that little rodent. Considering that guinea pigs only lived about four years, I thought it was ironic that she might actually outlive me.

Still nothing was coming from the council side of the table. I expected our parents to scream, shout, even cry to get us to change our minds. I didn't expect what happened next.

"What the hell," Pete spoke up in his gravelly voice. "I've been wanting to retire for years."

"It's not like we need the money . . ." Montgomery ventured timidly.

The others looked at one another, then turned to us and nodded simultaneously.

"Right," York said. "Tradition is so overrated."

We stared at them as if at some point they were all going to burst into flames. That would have surprised us less than the words that came out of their mouths.

"You're serious?" Gin squeaked.

Her mother nodded. "Why not? I want to spend more time with my grandchildren, not stuck on this island handing out death sentences."

The others seemed to agree. Was this for real? How did that happen? We weren't even that persuasive.

Dak eyed them suspiciously. "You mean I can stop training Louis? And I never have to train Sofia?"

Carolina snorted. "Like I want that precious little girl to kill people! Now, that doesn't mean she won't be taught how to fend for herself."

We watched in awe as the council stood up and made small talk. This had really happened. Without bloodshed. Holy shit.

My cousins hugged their respective parents, who in return hugged them back. Mum came over to me and threw her arms around my neck. After a few seconds, I held her. It was over. It was—

Zzzzzzzzzzzzzzzzt.

And in a split second, the Bombay Council lay twitching on the floor. I knew Missi had something rigged up with the last council where she zapped them at a crucial moment. But I'd never seen it. It was somewhat disturbing to watch our sixty-plus-year-old parents twitching like lobotomized electric eels at our feet.

"Missi!" Liv screamed. "You were only supposed to do that as a last resort!" She ran to help her father up.

Missi shrugged. "When was I ever going to get to do it now that we're going legit? Besides, these bastards just put me through a month of unmitigated hell for a stupid reason." She smiled innocently. "A girl's gotta have a little fun now and then."

It was over. Four millennia of wet work were over without so much as a whimper. How about that? I might have waxed more philosophical on it if I didn't have a planeload of turbulence waiting for me on the tarmac.

I left the others to negotiate the terms of the dissolution of the company and made my way to the plane. And even though we had just scored a major victory without spilling so much as one drop of blood, my mood worsened with each step.

Ronnie had something to say. No doubt it was that she had chosen Drew over me. Perhaps she'd twist the knife and tell me why him. Whatever it was, this was going to be unpleasant.

I found her sitting alone on the steps of the jet. I didn't want to talk to her. But since I'd just dragged her into another hemisphere, I guess I owed her something.

"Hey," she said.

"Come on. We can take you two home now." I took her hand to lead her up the steps but she pulled out of my grip.

"You are so wrong about me." She wasn't pleading. She just wanted me to know.

I cocked my head to the side. "Am I?"

She nodded. "You never gave me a chance to explain. And I'm really pissed off about that."

"Well, the feeling's mutual, because you didn't try to explain." My brain hurt. I wanted to go home, sleep for a week, then think all this through.

"Okay. I guess that's somewhat true," Ronnie said after a moment.

"Well, here's your big chance. Go ahead. Explain it."

For a second I thought she was going to get angry and refuse to talk.

"Drew isn't my boyfriend."

"What?" Not a great response, but considering the month I'd had, it was a respectable one.

"He isn't my boyfriend."

"Oh. Right." I'd had enough of this. If she wanted to play games I had Risk and Sorry on the plane.

"He's gay. And he's my cousin," Ronnie said, a slight glimmer of victory in her eyes.

"Right. And the Victorian house is really several apartments." Oh, that nasty sarcasm.

"No, Drew is house-sitting for a professor who is on sabbatical in Paraguay. My apartment is being renovated due to an asbestos problem."

Oh. Shit. I had hated her over asbestos.

"You never gave me the chance to explain," she concluded. "If you had, you would've known that."

I didn't say anything, so of course she decided it was a good idea to continue.

"What is it with you men, anyway? All I've learned

from being around you that no matter how well educated and worldly, you are still jealous, possessive and love to fight. You jump to conclusions at a moment's notice and never stop to think about it—"

"Maybe you're right," I cut her off. It was too painful to hear that she had such a low opinion of me. Hell, I had a low opinion of myself.

"And then, after dumping me unceremoniously without so much as an explanation, you leave. And a few weeks later, you show up again with a file full of . . ." The words choked in her throat. "Full of ugly things I'd rather not have known, thank you." She paused. "You came by just to hurt me even more. Just to prove you were right. And then you left, again, without allowing me to explain."

Somehow, Veronica had managed to make herself really angry at me all over again. And I just stood there and let her.

She pushed past me and climbed aboard the jet. We didn't speak all the way back to Cedar Rapids.

Chapter Thirty-four

"Each success only buys an admission ticket to a more difficult problem."

—HENRY KISSINGER

The first thing I did was put an unconscious Dekker on the family plane. He awoke on the tarmac in Amsterdam without knowing how he got there. I left him a letter in his pocket and hoped I would never see him again.

The next few weeks were a blur. I helped my cousins dismantle the Bombay Corporation. Our other cousins seemed relieved that we had done this without them. Paris and I managed to liquidate our assets and divide them equally among the living Bombays. We kept the island and the jet. We're not complete fools.

Missi got married to the guy she met on the reality show. I gave her a felted bag I knitted from the cashmere I got in Mongolia. For some reason, Missi and Lex spent their honeymoon in Ulaanbaatar before settling on Santa Muerta.

Life was slowly getting back to normal. Sartre grew fat as I spoiled her rotten with an extra ration of fruits and vegetables. I could tell she missed Ronnie. She actually seemed a little depressed.

I missed Ronnie. But I'd messed that woman up. Because of me, she'd eaten testicle soup, been kidnapped by a Dutch mercenary, saw her hero crucified and had a lover who treated her like a grand inquisitor. Maybe I was never meant to have a relationship. So why did I still believe that I could have had that with her? But what kind of relationship had areas that you could never, ever discuss? I'd lied to her about Dekker—letting her wonder what happened to him. And there was so much more about me she could never, ever know. Love couldn't last in a vacuum.

Somehow I managed to get in on the last few carnivals of the season. The work was steady. Some of the bloom was off the rose. I'd be forty in a year and a half. The injuries I'd suffered on the steppes of Mongolia still haunted me. And for the first time in my life, it seemed important that I had a plan for the next forty years.

That disturbed me the most. After all, I had taken so much joy from the idea that I was completely and utterly free. You know what started to get to me first? Eating alone. No, eating alone in a trailer, night after night. Suddenly the things I loved about my life had become the things I hated about my life.

Oh, sure, I toyed with the idea of settling down in some obscure university town. It wouldn't be too hard for me to land an academic job. But the thought of that made me feel sick inside. Was that insane or what?

As if I could settle down somewhere. And there it was. Whenever that possibility crossed my mind, I thought of Veronica. And when I thought of Veronica, I wondered what she was doing. Probably thinking evil thoughts about me. She probably was afraid I would show up on her doorstep again someday and kick her puppy.

With a sigh as rusty as the metal safety bar on the Ferris wheel, I snapped the two riders into place. It was a young couple, probably in their early twenties. I gave them a smile as I pulled the lever and sent them up to the moon.

"Poor thing," I heard as they came around the first time. I was bored or I wouldn't have been eavesdropping.

"He'll never amount to much," they said on their second rotation. Were they talking about me? No. It was stupid of me to even think that. They could be referring to anyone here.

"I love you," the woman said to the man on their third rotation, and I watched as they kissed, disappearing into the stars. Just for fun, I let them ride twice as long.

"Coney!" I turned to find Chudruk standing directly behind me.

I threw my arms around him in a big bear hug. "When did you get back to the States?"

Chudruk grinned. "I came with Zerleg. He starts college this semester!"

"That's great! He's going to Yale, right?" I ignored the fact that the Ferris wheel was still turning. I didn't hear anything anymore as the lovers went by.

"No. He decided on Iowa. Got a poetry scholarship."

I wasn't upset. Zerleg should go to the school he wanted to. I was just happy he got away from home to do what he loved.

We chatted for a while. Yalta was coaching Zolbin for next year's competition. Sansar-Huu and Odgerel had moved their family into town for the winter. It was comforting. Like mail from home.

Funny. I'd never thought of anyplace as home before. The mere sensation of thinking of Mongolia as home was electric. Man, I had it bad. The events of the summer meant that life was never going to be the same.

"So what happened to Ronnie?" Chudruk asked.

"Oh. We kind of went our separate ways."

Chud smiled. "Zerleg and I stopped to see her. She's going to help him get acclimated."

That got my attention. "Really? How is she?"

"She said you are a dick."

"Great." My enthusiasm waned a bit. So she still hated me. At least I inspired passion in her for something. Granted, it wasn't what I'd hoped, but at least it was something.

I had a break coming up, so we continued our conversation in the beer tent.

"How did you find me?" I said as I cracked open a bottle.

He shrugged. "It wasn't hard. I knew your patterns. I think you've ended every season at this fair."

"So are you coming back to work?" I asked him.

Chudruk shook his head. "No. I'm too old for this kind of crap."

A stab of pain in my shoulder made me think the same thing. "What are you going to do?"

"Oh," he said as he peeled the label off his bottle. "I've got a girlfriend in Paris. She's a surgeon. I figured we'd settle down. Have a couple of kids."

"Seriously? When did you get a French doctor girlfriend?" Seriously! When did that happen?

"There's a lot about me you don't know," Chud said with a wink. "You really shouldn't compartmentalize people. It's demeaning."

I stared at my friend and his sudden command of the English language.

"You've been holding out on me."

He shook his head. "No. You only saw what you wanted to see and didn't ask any more than that."

The news hit me like a one-ton weight. That was what Ronnie had said. Was I really like that?

I spent the evening in my trailer, completely freaked out. Oh, my God. I'd been doing what I accused others of doing. I was a hypocrite, an asshole and possibly a pseudointellectual. What was wrong with me?

"Sartre," I said as I strapped the seat belt over her cage at midnight. "This isn't going to work out."

The pig *wheek*ed her disapproval as I drove east. Somehow I was starting to think that she was smarter than me. And I didn't mind a bit.

Chapter Thirty-five

"Politics are very much like war. We may even have to use poison gas at times."
—Winston Churchill

The great thing about the way I lived my life was that I could walk away anytime I wanted to. Anytime things got inconvenient or uncomfortable, I could bolt. I told myself that was exactly what I wanted. My friends and family seemed to admire that about me.

But the truth was, I became the world's biggest loser. While they admired me, my family lived differently. And I never figured that out. Until now. What did I learn? That with all my prestigious degrees and vast worldwide travel, I really knew nothing at all.

Okay, I did know something. I knew that I was madly in love with Veronica Gale. And I knew that I had to see her and tell her the truth. About everything. What she did with the information was up to her. But I couldn't pursue her without her knowing the truth. All of it.

I pulled into a Target parking lot this time. It was three in the morning and I felt like a change was in order. I fell asleep with Sartre next to me. For the first time in a long time, I slept well.

I slept until the afternoon the next day. After renting a car—I didn't want to violate zoning ordinances by trying to park my trailer on a residential street—I drove to where she was staying and knocked on the door.

"Cy!" She actually looked happy to see me. Was this a trap? I was used to traps.

"Come in." Ronnie pulled on my sleeve and, once I was inside, stuck her hand into my jacket pocket and pulled out Sartre. She knew where I kept her. She knew that I'd brought her. Maybe there was something to the idea of fate after all.

"I need to talk to you," I said as I followed her into a large sunroom. We sat on the couch, facing each other.

"Okay. But first I have to tell you something." She took a deep breath. "Sartre just peed on me."

I looked down at her T-shirt and saw a large, spreading yellow stain. I think the pig winked at me.

Ronnie jumped up and ran out of the room. I toyed with suggesting she just take off her shirt, but thought maybe we should talk first. In a minute, she returned with a fresh shirt and Sartre wrapped up in a towel.

"I gave her a bath." She patted the little rodent's head. Sartre really looked pissed. Her fur was fluffed out, giving her the appearance of being much larger than she was, and the way her hair was askew gave her an angry look.

"Okay. So, I wanted to tell you that I'm sorry,"

Ronnie said with a grin. "I should have introduced you to Drew. I should have e-mailed you and explained when I didn't at the house. The thing is"—she chewed her lip adorably—"you are a dick and an asshole."

I nodded. "I know. You are absolutely right."

"And you make me so angry I want to kill something," she continued, without understanding the irony of her words. And why would she? I'd never told her.

"I'm not sure I can forgive you. Which is in direct conflict with my feelings for you."

I looked at her. "Why would you have any feelings for me? I don't deserve them. I treated you badly, thought I had you all figured out. I'm just here to apologize."

I stood and Ronnie grabbed my hand, pulling me back down to the couch. "That is exactly what I wanted to hear."

"It is?"

"Yes. I don't know why I'm telling you this, but I've realized that, in spite of my better judgment, I'm in love with you, Coney Bombay."

My head felt light and dizzy. It was a strange feeling when someone you loved told you they loved you too. My heart tightened in my chest, and I was worried about having a heart attack.

"What did you want to tell me?" she asked sweetly.

Oh. That. Now that she loved me, I didn't really want to tell her.

"The truth," I finally said. "I want you to know who I really am."

Ronnie shook her head. "I'm not pigeonholing you. And we have our whole lives to learn about each other."

Something in her light tone made me almost chicken out. But I was here and I had to say it.

"I'm an assassin."

She laughed. That was unexpected.

"No. Seriously. That's what I do. Or did, rather. I don't do it anymore."

Ronnie's mouth formed a perfect O. "You're serious?"

I nodded.

"You mean you aren't an overeducated carney?"

"No, I'm those things too. It's just that I also used to kill people."

She narrowed her eyes. "Define 'used to.'"

I guess if I was going to tell her everything, I should be completely honest. "As in up until a few weeks ago."

Ronnie got up and left the room. She was gone so long I was starting to think I should find the door on my own with my wet pig in tow.

Just as I was about to get up, she came back in carrying a bottle of red wine and two glasses. "I'm lousy at opening these things. Do you think we'll need another bottle?"

I poured. "No, one bottle should do it." And then I told her the story of my family and what the Bombay family business was all about.

Veronica listened carefully; her face did not betray one iota of emotion. Perhaps she had distanced herself, listening academically to what I had to say.

As the words came out of my mouth, I felt something strange. My shoulders started to relax. Tension flowed out of my arms into the sofa. I realized that I'd never told another non-Bombay about this. And what a burden it had been to carry it around all these years.

That was good. But the jury was still out on how Veronica would take the news. There was no guarantee she wouldn't throw me out on my ass. I didn't think she'd call the police. At least, I hoped she wouldn't.

We finished the bottle as I finished my story. I took a deep breath and waited for her to speak.

"That is so interesting," Ronnie said finally. "I mean, that really appeals to the anthropologist in me. And if I look at it that way, it doesn't bother me."

"It doesn't?"

She shook her head. "At least, not yet. Give me a few days."

"Oh." What else could I say?

"You only killed bad people, right?" The ring of hope in her voice was unmistakable.

I nodded. There was no point in telling her that I might have killed someone who didn't deserve to die. The cousins and I had vowed that we didn't want to know the truth about that, and I felt comfortable in my ignorance.

"Did you kill Dekker?"

"No. I couldn't do it. But I did drive him to thoughts of suicide." I told her the story of how I kept him alive as my own imprisoned therapist.

Ronnie snorted. "Oh, my God. That is the funniest thing I ever heard! Did you really do that?"

Okay. So it was all out there. And she took it well. But I still felt very uneasy.

"I shouldn't have accused you of anything," I started. "I was the one who pigeonholed you. I should have asked you—"

Ronnie silenced me with a kiss. She stood and started to pull me upstairs. I followed. Even though she hadn't fully processed everything and was very likely in total shock, I wasn't about to turn her down.

Chapter Thirty-six

Man: How you doing, Keaton?
Keaton: I can't feel my legs . . . Keyser.
                                    —*THE USUAL SUSPECTS*

So this was what it was like. I listened to Ronnie breathing beside me and sighed. If she woke up and decided she never wanted to see me again, at least I had this moment. I rolled over and watched the sun set lower in the sky. I wanted every late afternoon to be like this.

"Hey." Ronnie tapped me on the shoulder and I turned to face her, brushing a strand of hair from her eyes.

"Hey. How are you handling this?"

"Aside from the dream I had where you had a contract to take out an evil capybara, I'm okay."

"Really?" It was amazing how much hung in the balance of that one word.

"Really." She kissed me and climbed out of bed, starting to put her clothes on.

"Why are you putting your clothes on?" Why was she putting her clothes on? Maybe she didn't accept this like I thought.

"Don't be so paranoid!" Ronnie laughed as she threw my shirt at me. "Sartre and I are starving."

We made our way down to the kitchen and in moments we had a buffet of unrelated food, from cheese to Jell-O. Sartre had blueberries.

"So, you are okay with this?" I asked again, in danger of becoming annoying.

She nodded. "If I look at it from a scientific viewpoint, yes. And it helps that you only killed really bad people and have retired from the business altogether." She popped a grape into her mouth.

"I didn't expect it, is all. I thought you'd go through the roof."

Ronnie thumped me on the chest. "That's because you pigeonholed me."

"Yeah, I guess I did." We continued eating.

"So, are you ever going to tell me who killed Kennedy?" she asked.

I shook my head. "No, I can't do that. I had to sign a confidentiality oath in my own blood when I was five."

Her eyes went wide. "Really?"

I nodded.

"Wow. But there really was a conspiracy, right?"

I laughed. "Yes. While there isn't always a conspiracy, there was in that case."

Ronnie cocked her head to one side. "I bet you think I'm a real idiot over the whole Senator Anderson thing, don't you?"

I stiffened. "No. I don't."

She waved me off. "I mean, when you gave me that file listing all the horrible things Anderson had done, I was really mad at you. But I did some more digging and found out you were right. I guess I didn't look hard enough because I didn't want to believe that he'd really had a heart attack."

"Ronnie—"

"And the ridiculous lengths I went to in order to find his killer! And I was part of that weird group! We were so sure we were going to bring the senator's killer to justice!" She laughed again. "I mean, how do you bring something like heart disease to justice?"

"Ronnie." Something in my voice must have told her to stop, because she did. "You weren't wrong. Senator Anderson was killed for selling a list of CIA agents to Iran."

"What?" She slammed her hand down on the table, causing Sartre to jump. "Oh, my God! I was right!"

"You were right."

She started pacing wildly around the kitchen. "Oh, my God! He really was murdered! I can't believe it! Well, actually that is a relief, because I thought I might be nuts." She continued her inane prattle as she prowled around the room.

"And I bet you know it because you are in the business! Talk about weird shop talk! Can you tell me who did it?"

I nodded.

"Really? 'Cause you can't tell me about Kennedy! Really? Wow! This is like *The X-Files*!" She paused for a second, and I wondered if I would need a geek intervention here. "So, who was it? Who killed Anderson?"

The woman I loved looked at me with eyes shining, as if she had discovered the tomb of Jesus Christ.

"Me."

Chapter Thirty-seven

"An ideal form of government is democracy tempered with assassination."

—Voltaire

A number of years back, I scored a strange assignment: a young, idealistic senator from the Midwest. I have to admit, it took me by surprise. Anderson seemed like a good guy. That was, until I read the dossier.

Senator William Anderson was a sinner in saint's clothing. How he managed to keep everything under wraps, I'll never know. Actually, calling him a sinner is a bit of an understatement.

Do you remember that Stephen King book about the guy who could see the future? He saw that the guy running for president, a guy everyone loved and respected, was going to become a ruthless dictator responsible for the deaths of millions . . . in the future. In the end he decided he had to kill this man before he took office and tossed the nation into chaos and death.

It was kind of like that. Anderson wasn't just into hookers, corruption and graft. It was much worse.

The man had scams in third-world countries that would make you commit suicide. I won't go into a litany of his crimes here. Suffice it to say that the man was a monster.

However, he was a beloved public figure. So his death had to be out of my normal scope. I managed (I can't tell you how) to break into his house and discover he had a bum ticker. Missi drugged his toothpaste so that when he went to sleep that night, he went to sleep forever. It was clean and it was quick. And it looked like natural causes.

That was how I killed Senator William Anderson.

"Wow," was all Ronnie said when I told her. "Wow."

When she didn't speak for an hour, I collected Sartre and let myself out, carefully locking the door behind me.

Back in my trailer, I lay on my bed and cried. It was the first time I could remember doing that. I didn't just cry because I'd probably lost Ronnie and my chance at true love forever. I cried because I'd killed all those people since I was fifteen. I cried because my wanker brother was dead. I even cried because, in a couple of years, even Sartre would leave me. That's right, I premourned her death.

The sobbing shook my whole body, and after a few hours every muscle, even the one that controlled my thumb, ached. After splashing cold water on my face and taking some ibuprofen, I went to bed and slept.

I don't know how long I was asleep. I didn't feel very rested, but someone was pounding on my door. I threw on some clothes (you can't have a good long cry with clothes on) and opened the door to find my mother standing there.

"Squidgy!" She hurried into the trailer and shut the door. "You look like hell! Are you all right?"

"How did you find me?" I asked as I opened a Diet Coke and offered it to her. I poured myself one.

"Oh, we still have our ways," she said. "What happened here? Is Sartre all right?"

I nodded. "Nothing, Mum. I just got dumped by a woman I thought I had a real thing with because she found out I killed her idol. How are you?"

Mum reached up and gingerly touched my swollen face. "You've been crying! I've never known you to do that over a girl!"

"Yeah, well, she was special."

"Why did you tell her you killed whoever it was you killed?"

It was a fair question. "Because she had to know. Because I'm an idiot."

I sat there while my mother made me breakfast. She sat and watched as I ate.

"Why did you ask me to bring in Veronica Gale, Mum?"

She looked as though she didn't know what I was talking about.

"There's more to this than the council let on. I

didn't bring up my suspicions to the cousins, if that's what you are worried about."

Her face softened. "You got the assignment because I thought you were ready for it."

"What the hell does that mean? How was I ready for it? I kept Dekker alive to listen to my rants on Veronica! Clearly I wasn't ready for another assignment."

Mum nodded. "Which is why you were selected. We chose you to test because we knew you would fight us. We didn't ask you to kill Veronica—just to bring her in for questioning."

"What the hell?" My head ached as if I had a hangover. I tried to focus. Mum waited patiently.

"You wanted us to quit! You wanted out too!" I slapped the table.

She nodded. "Yes, we did. You got it!"

"You played us!" It wasn't Ronnie who had manipulated me—it was my mother! "Why?"

Georgia Bombay sighed heavily, and I saw for the first time that she was old. "You know, my generation tried to get out of the business before you were born."

Suddenly I was wide-awake. "You never told me. What happened?"

"Oh . . ." She waved her hand dismissively. "We were children of the sixties—very antiestablishment. The council represented the Man. We didn't want to kill. We wanted peace."

An image of the council members as hippies invaded my brain. I shuddered.

"Unfortunately, as you know, our parents' generation was much more hard-core. They came from the generation of the Great War between good and evil. Everything was black-and-white to them. They were convinced that carrying on the tradition was their way of saving the world."

"Damn. I would've liked to see you take on the council." And I wanted to too. That had to be something to see.

"We have it somewhere on film. I think Pete kept a copy. The council recorded everything back then. They were pretty paranoid."

I took a moment to wrap my mind around this. It was an incredible shock.

"But our folks wouldn't hear of disbanding the organization. They didn't want to kill us either, so they agreed to pretend it never happened if we went back to work. Which we did."

"I can't believe this." I really couldn't. "So you set us up to bring down the company."

"Yes! And it worked brilliantly too! I'm quite the actress, wouldn't you say? York wanted to hold out a little longer—you know, add some more drama to make it fun. But Pete couldn't hold off anymore."

Make it fun? Okay. I could understand that.

"And it was fun finally giving it all up once and for all. Well, except for when Missi electrocuted us. That sort of sucked, dear."

I grinned. "I guess it sort of did." So it was all a ruse. How about that. Who would have thought my mother was capable of such surprises?

"Well, I really should be going, honey. They are all waiting for me."

"Who is?"

"The rest of the council. We're heading to Greenland to tell our parents."

I frowned. "What if they don't like the idea?"

She smiled. "Well, I guess they will just have to stay at that nursing home then, won't they?" With a wink, she was gone.

Chapter Thirty-eight

Blue Raja: Your boy's a limey fork-flinger, Mother.
  What will the bridge club say?
Blue Raja's Mother: You need more forks?
  —MYSTERY MEN

My cell rang the moment the door closed. The caller ID said, *Veronica Gale, 27, grad student at the University of Iowa, a bit anal-retentive about anthropology.* I didn't know how Missi did that.

"Hello." I didn't really know what to say. Me! The man who always had something pithy to say.

"Why did you leave?"

"You weren't speaking." To me that seemed like a demand to get out of her life forever. But maybe that was just me.

"Where are you now?" She sounded a little frantic. Was she worried I had left the state? That would be nice.

I gave her directions and, to my surprise, she hung up on me. Ten minutes later I was not so surprised when she knocked on my door.

"So this is where you live?" She wandered around, opening cupboards and poking into things. "It's nice."

"Thanks."

"And you look awful. Like you were crying or got punched in the face."

"Yeah. I know."

"Well, which was it?" she demanded.

"Crying." I was man enough to admit that. Or was I? I wasn't really sure what kind of man I was anymore. And that came as a shock.

Veronica plucked Sartre from my bed and sat down holding her. "Why did you say you'd help me?"

"What?" I missed something.

"Why did you say you would help me find Anderson's killer if you knew it was you?"

That was a fair question. "You were so passionate about it. I wanted to help you."

"Did you think you would ever tell me the truth?"

"I have no idea."

"Really?"

"Really. I had no idea where this would lead. I guess I just thought I'd see where the wind took me."

Veronica thought about that for a moment. "Kind of like your life, huh?"

I nodded. She was right.

"I like your RV. Is this where we will live?"

I sat down out of shock. "What are you saying?"

She shook her head like I was clueless. "It's either this or my asbestos-infested apartment. That professor is coming back from Paraguay soon."

"You . . . you want to live with me?" I actually stuttered. That had to be a first.

"Yes, Coney Bombay. I want to live with you. I want to make an honest man out of you and be a mother to your guinea pig."

"Wow. That's a good offer." I smiled. "Okay. You can live here."

Ronnie closed the gap between us, wrapping her arms around my neck and kissing me in a way that made my hair stand on end.

"Okay. I'll get my stuff. Just one thing."

I kissed her again. It felt like home. "And what is that?"

She smiled. "I really hate the nickname Ronnie."

Epilogue

And so it came to pass that the Bombays were out of the assassination business. This was big news, but there was no one we could really tell. Mum's visit to Greenland with the others went well. The previous council members had had enough of pureed food and the sullen staff. They all retired to Santa Muerta to live out the rest of their days in peace. I think they even liked it.

My cousins were thrilled with their early retirement. No one really had to work ever again, due to our trust funds. But I did hear a rumor about Paris and Dak opening a marketing consulting firm. We all visit our island from time to time, for real vacations now. Missi took down the ropes course in what she called "a ritualistic cleansing with fire." I'm not sure what that was all about.

Mum and Dad took a trip around the world to celebrate. By the time they came back one year later, Veronica and I presented them with their first grandson, named Theodore. He was the first Bombay without a place-name. My parents bought an RV so they could travel with us wherever we went. This was annoying at first, until we realized how difficult it was to find sitters when you didn't know where you were.

Sartre appeared to like the new addition to the

family. She seemed a bit honored, if guinea pigs could be honored, that we gave the baby her name for his middle name. As for Veronica and me, we decided that we were just going to travel around the country, checking things out here at home. We figured we had five years to find the place we would want to settle down before Theodore had to start school. My mother is rooting for New Mexico, but I kind of like San Francisco. Dad is still trying to convince us to move to Australia, and, according to Veronica, no matter where we go, Iowa is the best place to be.

Who knows where we will end up? I'm not making any plans yet. I am looking forward to settling down with my family . . . someday. And for a retired carney/assassin with a guinea pig and a Ph.D., the future looks pretty good.

ELISABETH NAUGHTON

Antiquities dealer Peter Kauffman walked a fine line between clean and corrupt for years. And then he met the woman who changed his life—Egyptologist Katherine Meyer. Their love affair burned white-hot in Egypt, until the day Pete's lies and half-truths caught up with him. After that, their relationship imploded, Kat walked out, and before Pete could find her to make things right, he heard she'd died in a car bomb.

Six years later, the woman Pete thought he'd lost for good is suddenly back. The lies this time aren't just his, though. The only way he and Kat will find the truth and evade a killer out for revenge is to work together—as long as they don't find themselves burned by the heat each thought was stolen long ago . . .

STOLEN HEAT

ISBN 13: 978-0-505-52794-3

✂ ☐ YES!

Sign me up for the Love Spell Book Club and send my FREE BOOKS! If I choose to stay in the club, I will pay only $8.50* each month, a savings of $6.48!

NAME: _____

ADDRESS: _____

TELEPHONE: _____

EMAIL: _____

☐ I want to pay by credit card.

☐ VISA   ☐ MasterCard.   ☐ DISCOVER

ACCOUNT #: _____

EXPIRATION DATE: _____

SIGNATURE: _____

Mail this page along with $2.00 shipping and handling to:
Love Spell Book Club
PO Box 6640
Wayne, PA 19087
Or fax (must include credit card information) to:
610-995-9274
You can also sign up online at **www.dorchesterpub.com**.
*Plus $2.00 for shipping. Offer open to residents of the U.S. and Canada only.
Canadian residents please call 1-800-481-9191 for pricing information.
If under 18, a parent or guardian must sign. Terms, prices and conditions subject to change. Subscription subject to acceptance. Dorchester Publishing reserves the right to reject any order or cancel any subscription.